The Magic in the P

'I risked everything to get you that water last
night. You don't realize how little we've got.
There's not a drop to be spared!' Johin shouted.
'You're a Sand boy, aren't you? Your people want
to steal our water. And now I've saved your life!'

The River Planet is in danger. Its life source,
the Lightwater River, is dying, poisoned through
centuries of pollution and misuse. Manny, a starving
and mysterious Sand boy, is the only person who
knows how to put things right. Now, through a
simple act of kindness, Johin is entwined in his
dangerous quest.

As they cross the drought-stricken land, Johin
realizes that the River offers life in more than one way.
But clearing its source won't be enough. She and
Manny also have to defeat the evil Brilliance.

Beth Webb lives in Somerset with her husband,
four children, one guinea pig, twelve goldfish and
a large number of white mice (one of whom is
called Nuffle).

The Magic in the Pool of Making *was written for my son Tom. One day, while watching the news, which as usual was about pollution, drought, famine and injustice, Tom asked, 'Why doesn't God do something?'*

This is the best answer I could think of.

The Magic
in the
Pool of Making

Beth Webb

A LION PAPERBACK
Oxford · Batavia · Sydney

Copyright © 1992 Beth Webb

Published by
Lion Publishing plc
Sandy Lane West, Oxford, England
ISBN 0 7459 2234 1
Albatross Books Pty Ltd
PO Box 320, Sutherland, NSW 2232, Australia
ISBN 0 7324 0557 2

First edition 1992

Acknowledgment
To the silk-purse makers

A catalogue record for this book is available
from the British Library

Printed and bound in Great Britain
by Cox & Wyman Ltd, Reading

Contents

Prologue: The Legend of the Lightwater   9

1   A Useless Find   11
2   A Magic of the Making   19
3   Brilliance   30
4   The Fox and the Goose   38
5   A Disastrous Escape   51
6   Manny's Song   58
7   Summons to Hogendam   62
8   Capture!   66
9   The Flying Mouse   76
10 Dream Song   83
11 Johin Alone   91
12 Risking the Magic   99
13 Greenhevel   104
14 The Moon on the Rocks   111
15 The Shadow of Brilliance   119
16 Hogendam   126
17 Hunger Mountain   130
18 Genadatown   138
19 The River Plays Fair   146
20 Shams and Imitations   152
21 The Depths of Darkness   162
22 The Words of Unmaking   173
23 Nuffle's Surprise   180
24 The Beginning   186

The Upper Reaches of the Lightwater River

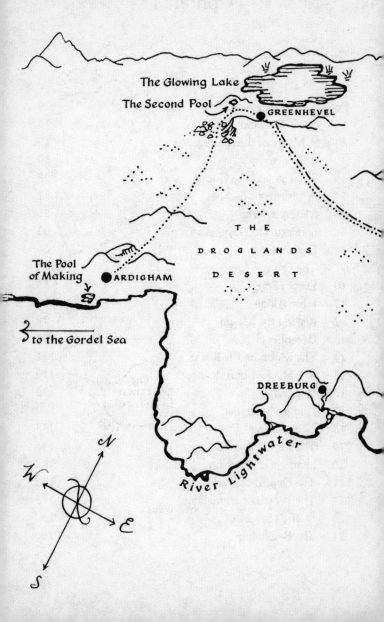

The Glowing Lake

The Second Pool

GREENHEVEL

THE

DROGLANDS

DESERT

The Pool
of Making

ARDIGHAM

to the Gordel Sea

DREEBURG

River Lightwater

N

W

E

S

BROTPLAIN

HOGENDAM

The
Dam

Heylebul Island

GENADATOWN

THE CITY

The Dump

The
Known
Source

River Lightwater

·········· Johin and Manny's route

—·—·—·— the main road

〰〰 rivers and waterways

∴·.∴· desert

♨ ♨ marshes

The Legend of the Lightwater

Strange tales are told of the River Planet, that tiny green-and-blue world, so far away, yet so like our own.

In the morning of time, the Maker smiled at his reflection of Light within the great River. He stretched out his hand, and from a small pool at the flood's edge, he fashioned his likeness from the rich red-black mud on the bottom. These Mud people would be shapers, like himself.

Then, from the shallow sandy eddies, he formed a paler Sand people, reflecting his wisdom like a mirror.

These Mud and Sand people would always be together, always needing each other to complete the Light's true reflection.

With delight, the Maker watched this gentle planet blossom and become fruitful.

But as skills and words grew, the people changed. They became cunning and greedy. They ceased to wonder at the joyful Light within the River, and they turned to adore the glistening brilliance of their own achievements.

The stronger people made the weaker ones work hard. Long hours were filled with lifeless labour. The wise ones exchanged their songs for deceit and rhetoric.

They no longer sought the Light within the River to give them life. They controlled their own lives. Their makings and their words were very powerful.

Soon poisonous waste began to spoil the land and foul the rivers. Slowly, as the years turned, the soil died, and the waters failed. Even the great Lightwater, the widest, deepest and fastest river of them all, began to change.

The bright sparkle on the surface dimmed. Disease was born.

The Maker did not seem to care. Many said there never had been a Light within the River—it was so dull and slow.

The rains failed. The land died. The Mud people blamed the Sand people, and the Sand people blamed the Mud people. Everywhere was sorrow and grief.

The Mud people's Drought Council took charge of what water was left. Patrolling Water Guards decided who would drink and who would die. The Sand people fled to the deserts to sing their sorrow.

But the Maker saw their grief. Their pain was his pain. As he watched, rejected and forgotten, he whom they had once known as the Light within the River, stretched out his hand once more . . .

1
A Useless Find

Suddenly Johin tripped.

She had been so busy peering cautiously into the shadows, she had not noticed a thin boy lying motionless in the dry grass.

Johin was furious. All the fruit she had so carefully gathered in her skirt was squashed to a pulp. She scrambled up and turned on the boy. He was one of the Sand people. She kicked him, hard. He still didn't move. 'Good, he's dead,' she thought.

Then she heard a horrid rattling sound. She froze to the spot. It sounded like the tail of the deadly rock snake scraping the ground ready to strike.

Nothing stirred in the dust.

The noise came again . . . and again.

After several minutes of not daring to breathe, or even to blink away the fly on her eyelid, she realized it was not a snake, it was the boy's dry lungs gasping for air. She looked at him. His skin was pale and flaking and his lips were black and swollen. Most of his brown hair had snapped off already. He wore a short kilt of goat-hair, like all his people, but the gold bangles were missing. His family must have sold them to buy water.

Johin looked at the boy lying helpless in the dust. He was a little older than herself, and terribly thin. She forgot to be angry, and began to feel sorry for him. He was only a boy.

He would die soon if she did not get him a drink, but the Drought Council's penalty for stealing water was death ... And it would be certain death for *her* if she was caught helping one of the terrible Sand people. They were enemies and thieves. For weeks now there had been rumours of hordes of them gathering in the hills ready to attack the town and steal the last of the water.

She must get him back to his family. They must care for their own. That was the best she could do, but it was dangerous enough.

He was tall, but so wasted she could lift him easily.

His family could not be far away. Sand people always stayed together. She staggered with her load from patch to patch of drought trees, peering through the blinding light for glimpses of Sand people. But, apart from a few vultures wheeling overhead, there was nothing.

At last she collapsed, exhausted. She too would soon die at this rate. The drought tree under which they were resting was carrying a few fruit. She picked one and tore at the skin with her teeth. She took a bite, but she could not swallow it.

The boy's breathing sounded painful. His eyes flickered open and looked at her, without expression.

Not quite knowing why, she picked a tiny morsel from the fruit, and pushed it into the boy's mouth. To her amazement, he swallowed it. Slowly, piece by piece, she fed him the whole fruit, then another. His breathing slowed, and he slept. She found more for herself, and thought. If she left him here, wild animals would kill him. If she took him home, he would be shot.

She screwed up her eyes against the blazing sun and surveyed the cliff face which rose steeply behind them. It was riddled with caves. Thousands of years ago, her ancestors had lived there. If she could get him inside a cave, he might be safe.

It did not take her long to spot one that would be easy to reach. She picked the boy up again. The walk was slow and painful. He seemed to weigh more with every step she took.

At last they reached the cave. It looked safe enough. At least it was cool in there. Johin gathered dry leaves and made a bed. 'I'll have to make you a fire,' she said. 'That's illegal at the moment in case it spreads, but if I don't, the jackals will get you . . . not that there's much on you to eat.'

The boy nodded weakly, and watched expressionless as she cracked flints together over a small pile of dust-dry twigs. Lighting a fire was all too easy.

'I'll see if I can find someone to take care of you. The fire will protect you while I'm gone, but first I need a rest too.'

She leaned back against the cave's cool rock walls and felt in her pocket for her mouse, Nuffle. He squeaked with delight and ran up her arm and settled under her chin.

Johin smiled and stroked his creamy white fur with her little finger. 'I bet you're thirsty, aren't you?' she said. 'When my head has stopped spinning, I'll see what I can do.'

She could always think better with Nuffle under her chin, and now she needed to think.

So much had happened since that morning. She had been playing her favourite game of being a cat. The feeling of fear and tension all around suited her. Pretending that the Sand people were watching her every move, she had worked her way up the steep slopes behind the town. Leaping from shadow to shadow, she reached the patchy shade of what had once been the great forest. It was now a desert scattered with a few dead trunks and rough copses of 'drought trees' which seemed to thrive whatever the weather.

She had hoped that a few of these might have some fruit: a hard-skinned apple. Anything was a pleasant change from stale bread and stringy meat. To her delight there was plenty of fruit. The terrible heat and the fear of the Sand people must have kept the other townsfolk at home. She did not mind the heat, and she was not scared of Sand people.

Using her tunic skirt as a bag, she soon had enough for a feast. Deep in her pocket, Nuffle munched happily on a handful of wild grass seeds.

All the time she watched for the slightest movement among the rocks which might betray a group of Sand people. But she had not watched where she put her feet. Now she was in a fix.

'Will you get me some water, please?' came a sudden, rasping voice.

'Water?' she gasped, jerking out of her reverie. 'Isn't it enough that I've saved your useless life? You want *me* to risk the death penalty to get *you* water? You Sand people are so selfish! What about *me*? I could be shot!'

The boy turned over on his prickly bed and lay still. Johin watched him for some time, then, making up the fire, she quietly slipped out of the cave. She ran back down into the town, picking a few more drought fruit as she went, to explain her long absence.

After supper she casually said, 'Fellina has asked me to stay tonight. Is that all right?' Her mother looked sad, but nodded. 'I never see you these days, Johin. Why don't you ever want to stay at home with us?'

Johin pouted. 'It's stifling here. I don't know why you don't suffocate. Come out into the hills with me, it's much fresher.'

Her mother looked languidly out at the quivering, purple horizon. 'It's too hot. I can't move. It's dangerous up there, anyway. I do wish *you* wouldn't go, Johin, but I'm too exhausted to stop you.' She sighed and smiled. 'Go and stay with Fellina, but come home in the morning ... I do love you ...' her voice trailed weakly, chasing Johin's shadow out into the dusk.

Johin only stopped long enough at her friend's house to whisper the alibi and borrow an old green glass bottle. She knew her parents would be too hot and tired to check up on her. Anyone who had the energy could do more or less what they liked—as long as they did not cross the Water Guards.

She knew she did not really care about a useless Sand boy. But Johin loved adventures, and this was real, *and* dangerous.

She waited for dark in a quiet corner, then prowling with cat's feet as silent as velvet, Johin began to work her way through the town.

She tried not to think of what would happen if a Water Guard caught her. To calm her nerves, she tried to imagine what Ardigham must have been like in the days of water ... before the strangling fear and heat had taken hold.

The town had been elegant with tall stone buildings, but they were deserted and crumbling now. In the centre of the town square was a huge ornamental basin, carved around the rim with scenes from ancient legends. People said that once, water had been thrown high into the air from several large spouts on the basin floor. It had been called a fountain. Johin could not imagine such a thing.

Now the basin was dry and cracked, but in the middle stood a heavy black iron pump. Only the town elders and anyone rich enough to own a water pass could use it. Johin did not care. That water tasted stale anyway.

As she crept silently past the basin, she could see the black outline of a Water Guard next to the pump. The moon glistened on his gun as he turned at the slight sound of her footfall. She flattened herself against a huge stone lion and held her breath.

The guard shrugged, and she slipped into the steeply-stepped backstreets of the derelict town. In the moonlight, she could glimpse the cold brightness of the desert beyond.

Here, an ancient forest had once swept down the valley sides to swathe the town in a cool mantle of dark green and blue. The town had stood proudly on the banks of the River Blackwater, with great ships moored along the quay.

Now Ardigham was just a pile of dusty stones above a deep, empty canyon with a tiny trickle of water at the bottom. Townspeople clambered down the rocks twice a day to fill water carriers which they hauled with aching backs and blistered hands up to their little concrete shacks, well away from the town's dangerous ruins.

Johin could not risk the cliff path down to the river in the dark. It was too dangerous, and she was likely to get caught. Instead, she took a narrow track which led downhill and out of sight to a small pool. The guards patrolled there only occasionally, because the water was too muddy to drink.

Legend said that this was the very pool from which her people had been made when the Maker fashioned them in his likeness from the glossy red-black mud at the bottom. Not that anyone believed that sort of thing any more, but there *was* something special about the place, and although the river now ran far below, the pool had never quite dried.

Johin swallowed. The moon was covered by a dust cloud, making the pool look eerie as it lay silent and dark in a little hollow shaped like a hand. She stood motionless for a while, summoning all her courage. Why was she doing this anyway?

Suddenly the moon escaped its cloud, and Johin gasped. She had expected to find little more than a muddy puddle, but there, glimmering in the moonlight, was the pool, full and clear. Desperate for a drink, she bent over the smooth, cool water. It was as still and bright as glass. But instead of her own face, a large black cat looked back at her.

Terrified, she did not touch a drop. She swept the bottle through the water once. Without daring to look again, she ran.

As she scrambled up the dry rocks, her foot knocked a stone into the ravine. It echoed like a shot. The noise cracked again and again, loudly and clearly all along the hard rocky valley.

Johin ran frantically, unable to breathe, and choked with terror until she fell panting at the mouth of the boy's cave. The fire had gone out. He was alone and motionless. Was it too late?

Suddenly there came a short, harsh rasping sound. She froze and held her breath, peering out of the corner of her eye for a rock snake.

Silence.

Then again...

And again...

Gratefully she sucked in air and felt her legs go limp. It was the Sand boy. He was still breathing! Hoping desperately that the huge black cat had not followed her, she bent over the boy, and lifted his head up. Her heart was beating fast; she was very frightened.

'Listen!' she said urgently in his ear. 'You won't know this, because you are a Sand boy, but we, the Mud people, were made from the mud from the pool this water comes from. Our stories say that life is in the water itself. I don't know whether it's true or not, but you must drink!'

She immediately felt stupid for having told him of the

legend. 'What does he care about our folk tales?' she thought.

She held the heavy glass bottle to his lips. Nothing happened. He was too weak to drink.

She tried wetting her fingers and holding them to his lips. That was too little, and too much got spilt.

Frantically, she searched around the cave for something to use as a cup. Nothing.

At last she tore a strip from the skirt of her tunic and soaked it in water. She carefully squeezed the precious drops into the boy's open mouth. The rasping breaths were coming less and less frequently. Then, at last, he gulped.

All night, slowly, painstakingly, she gave him the water in the bottle. As the morning light crept slowly into the cave and the red moon waned, his breathing became regular, and he slept.

Johin lay back next to him, and stared, dazed and exhausted, at the roof of the cave. She was vaguely aware of Nuffle scurrying around the cave floor, licking at the few spilt drops of water. She was too tired to care.

Sleep came fitfully until a voice next to her said: 'You have had nothing all night. Drink.'

2
A Magic of the Making

Johin sat up in amazement.

The boy was smiling at her, holding out the bottle.

'It's all gone,' she said despondently.

'No it's not, see.'

She took the bottle. It was not full, but it was far from empty. She drank. It was the most delicious water she had ever tasted.

'It's funny, but I always thought the water from that pool was bitter and muddy,' she said.

'True,' said the boy, 'if you take it only for yourself. As you said, there *is* life in the water—but it has to be taken to be shared.'

'How do you know our stories?' she asked, angrily.

'We are River-born as well,' he replied quietly.

'What nonsense! Sand people were made in the desert! Look at you, you're all dry and yellow! *We* who are River-born are black and beautiful and moist. It is a sign of our birth and our chosen state.' She tossed her long shiny red-black hair, and glared at him contemptuously.

'Once the Great River flowed over this whole land,' the boy replied softly, almost singing. 'And the sand was formed by the wearing and motion of the River. Once there were many pools such as yours, and from them many peoples and beings were made. But they all come from the Maker's Light at the source of the Great River.'

He paused and looked at her. 'Tell me, how do you name your river?'

'The "Blackwater", of course. I'm surprised you don't know *that*, seeing you're so clever!' she snapped sarcastically.

'Once, in your tongue it was called the "Bleekwater", which meant the "Bright" or "Lightwater". But now, as the mud flows thick and black and greasy and only bloodsucking leeches grow in and around it, I am not surprised you call it the "Blackwater".'

'That proves you don't know what you're talking about,' she retorted. 'It's really good water!'

He looked at her sadly. 'I'm afraid it only shows you don't know how good the water *should* be. Before the drought and the poison, it was *alive*.'

Johin could think of no reply, and the boy sat silent for a while. Then he sighed and looked at her. 'I am much better, thanks to you, but I am in a hurry. I need more water. Will you go again, please?'

Johin sat bolt upright. Now she was *really* angry.

'What! I risked everything to get you that bottle of water last night. I was even chased by wild animals! You don't realize how little we've got. We are desperate. There's not a drop to be spared amongst ourselves, let alone for the likes of you!'

The boy looked so thin and pale, she felt sorry, but secretly she couldn't help hoping that he might feel better later and go for himself.

She hesitated. 'I might try again after dark, but then you must go back to your own people.'

'Who are they?' asked the boy, looking straight at her.

Johin was furious and terrified at the same time. 'You're a Sand boy, aren't you? There are hundreds of you up in the hills. You're coming to pounce on us and kill us in our sleep. You want to steal our water. We know you're there.

We've seen you! We're not stupid! And now I've saved your life! I must have been heat-crazed—unless it's some sort of evil magic you put on me! You Sand people are always doing things like that.'

She peered at him, suddenly afraid, and began to scramble towards the cave entrance. She hoped desperately that Nuffle was in her pocket. She did not want to have to stop and find him.

The boy held out his hand. 'My name is Manny,' he said.

She looked at his hand blankly for a few moments. 'I ... I'm Johin ...' she said hesitantly.

'Enemies give neither their hands nor their names,' smiled Manny. 'The Sand people are not the enemy. They are only thirsty. They are gathering in the hills hoping to beg water from your people. You will find the true enemy within your townspeople. Go to the pool and get me some more water, and you will see what I mean.'

Johin sat staring at him open-mouthed. 'Listen,' he said, laying a thin dry hand on her arm. 'You have tasted the water as it was meant to be drunk. How do you feel?'

'As it happens, wonderful,' she said warily.

'You have the Lightwater within you now, and it will protect you.' He wet his fingers with a little water and made a small sign in the dust on her forehead. It made her spine tingle with an icy delight.

'Is it magic?' she asked.

'Yes,' Manny replied, with a twinkle in his eye. 'I have given you the Mark of the River. It is a real magic, a magic of the Making, not just a showman's trick. You must understand, the Lightwater is *my* River...' he grinned in a way which made him look full of fun and very kind, '...and even the big black cats are mine, so don't be frightened.'

He looked straight at her, with deep green-blue eyes

that she could not escape. He said urgently, 'Please go. You'll know what to do when the time comes. Just listen to the River.'

'How do you know about the cat?' she asked suspiciously.

'You'll see when you get there,' he said with a grin. 'But she's not as frightening as she looks. Now please go. I am still very weak.'

Suddenly he called her back. 'You had better have your mouse, Johin. He's been sleeping under my chin.'

'Nuffle! You bad mouse!'

Excited, frightened and confused, Johin stroked her face against Nuffle's soft fur. He smelled so nice and safe. She slipped him back into her pocket and picked up the bottle.

Slowly and in a daze she retraced her steps of the night before. Sand people seemed to be everywhere—behind every rock and dry bush. Some were clutching a few pathetic belongings, and others were trying to comfort miserable children. Two or three babies had been laid on a goat-hair cloth in the shade of a drought tree. They were quite still. The strange chanting had ceased. The singers were too dry to breathe.

Without saying a word, Johin picked up three empty earthenware jars which were lying with a few sad remnants of baggage. Clutching the jars by the leather neck-loops, she set off down the hill.

The Sand people stared after her dumbly, but did not object.

Manny had been right, the evil was not here. Johin had seen neither weapons nor threats of any kind amongst the people. Just need.

As she approached the pool she heard voices. Silently she sank behind a rock to listen. She felt nervously in her pocket for Nuffle.

22

'I tell you, there's a change.'

'There can't be,' came a second voice. 'There's not been a drop of rain for years.'

Both men were Water Guards. One was Johin's cousin, Collim. He held a heavy-looking gun in his hand, and Johin knew him well enough to be sure that he would use it.

Collim was scratching his head. 'We'll have to report it. A pool that was empty yesterday is almost full today. I don't understand it.'

'If there's more,' said the second man, whom Johin only knew by sight, 'then no one would know and no one would tell if *we* had some. I'm desperately thirsty.'

Collim shrugged and said, 'On your own head be it. I'll say nothing.' And he strode off along the hot, red, dusty road towards the town.

The man stood looking at the water for a while, then he knelt down and lapped like a dog. 'My, that's bitter,' he said, 'but I needed it.'

Johin could see what Manny had meant. The water had strange effects on people. The man's face was beginning to look distinctly like that of a dog. She flattened herself against the rock, and watched, terrified.

At last, Collim, the Chief of the Water Guards and a couple of the town elders came sweating and panting down to the pool. The elders were short and fat, and they were using their white linen shawls of office to dab at the sweat running down their wobbly faces.

They rounded an outcrop of rock puffing and panting, and stood open-mouthed at the sight of the dog, with a ridiculously draped uniform trailing in the water. The creature stopped drinking, looked up and barked. Suddenly it shook itself free of the sodden uniform, and ran off.

'What was that?' asked the Chief Water Guard.

'It was wearing Sergeant Koos' uniform,' said Collim. 'We came up here together. If it was *him*, there must be some evil magic in the water.'

'It's bound to be a plot by the Sand people,' snarled the Chief, showing his pointed teeth. 'They've probably poisoned the water.'

'It's that strange singing, it's bad magic, mark my words,' said one of the elders, shaking his head.

Collim swallowed hard and looked sideways at his Chief, whom he had always privately likened to a crocodile.

Without knowing quite why she did it, Johin stood up and found herself speaking very fast. 'Please, I think I know something about this pool. I took some water last night for someone who was dying. When I came back this morning, the pool was almost full. I'm sure it's because I shared what we had.

'When you went down the hill, Collim, I saw Sergeant Koos drinking the water. That's when he turned into a dog. It really *was* him! I watched it all! I think it happened because he *stole* for himself. But it isn't just for us! The pool will only be full as long as we share the water with everybody!'

'What nonsense!' snapped the Chief Guard. 'She's confessed to water theft. Arrest her!' Before she could run, Collim had caught her and twisted her arms painfully behind her back.

'It's the truth!' she screamed. 'I know it is!'

The Chief Guard wasn't listening. He had found her collection of earthenware jars and a green glass bottle behind the rock where she had been hiding. 'She was planning more theft,' he yelled. 'Who was this for?' He grabbed her hair and jerked her head back, glaring into her eyes.

It was no good lying. She was doomed anyway. 'For

some Sand people. They are desperate.'

'Nonsense!' he snorted, 'they're just too lazy to go and look for their own water. If they are thirsty, it's their own fault.'

Then a nasty gleam came into the Chief's eyes. He laughed out loud. 'Make her drink. That will be a suitable punishment. She must be a spy for the Sand people. Let *her* prove the water isn't poisoned . . .'

Collim grabbed Johin's shoulders, forced her on to her knees, and pushed her face down into the water. Once more she glimpsed the reflection of a large black cat, where her own face should have been. She tried not to scream and thought of what Manny had told her.

'May the Lightwater help me,' she thought, terrified. 'I've got to prove the truth by drinking! I hope it will understand.'

After a few seconds she found herself pulled back and allowed to breathe. She took her chance and shouted, 'Let me speak!'

'No harm,' sneered the Chief. 'You'll be quiet enough as soon as you become a rat.'

'Let me fill my jars,' begged Johin. 'The pool is full, there's plenty to share with the Sand people today. If nothing happens to me, you'll know there's no harm in the water. If I change, then you can deliver it for me, and you will see the Sand people turn into animals too.'

The Chief nodded and grinned. He was going to enjoy his day's work. Now he knew the Sand people were so close and so weak, he could easily finish them off. He would be sure of an extra water ration as a reward for his work. 'Fair enough,' he said, and nodded to Collim.

Johin filled the jars to the brim. 'Now keep drinking,' snarled the Chief. 'Drink plenty, it's a hot day.'

She drank deeply. It tasted wonderful. Nothing happened. The elders looked bemused. 'Why isn't she changing?'

they demanded.

'Because I didn't take for myself. I only drank to prove the truth,' she said. 'It's as I told you.'

The Chief laughed his horrible laugh, baring all his jagged teeth. 'All this talk of magic and poisons is children's tales. We only have *her* word for what happened, after all. Sergeant Koos must have become heat-crazed, dumped his clothes, and gone off into the hills. I can't say I blame him! He won't be the first to have gone mad in this heat. That dog was just a stray!' And without more ado, the Chief lay on the ground and began to drink...

The crocodile that swam into the middle of the pool looked a little confused, but it soon settled into the red-black mud and dropped off into a contented doze.

The elders looked in amazement from the crocodile to each other. 'Did we see that?' one of them asked.

The other shook his head. 'The heat is definitely getting to us!' And together they staggered back into the town as fast as their fat legs would carry them.

Collim looked bemusedly from the crocodile to Johin, then at the retreating elders running back up the slope, wobbling and flapping all the way.

He shook his head. 'Look, what *is* happening? I don't like being told to arrest my own cousin. Nasty things happen in prison, you know,' he said with a glower.

'Have I ever told you a lie?' asked Johin, looking straight at him.

'Lots,' said Collim, settling down on the ground next to her. He pointed gleefully at the crocodile. 'I always said he'd make a good one,' he grinned. 'At least there'll be a permanent guard on the pool now.'

But Johin wasn't in a mood for resting or joking. She stood up and started pulling at Collim's arm. 'If I told you what was really happening, you would never believe me.

You've got to see for yourself. Come with me. Now.'

'I can't. I'm on duty!'

Johin looked critically at the crocodile wallowing and slopping happily in the warm glossy mud. '*He's* not going to stop you, he's almost asleep! Anyway, you're a Water Guard, aren't you? You've got to investigate this fully. Come on!' Again she tried to tug him to his feet. Although he was not tall, he was stocky and very strong, and she could not budge him.

Collim began to look angry. His thick black brows knitted down over his eyes. 'Where?' he demanded.

'We must take this water to the Sand people. These jars are too heavy for me now they're full. *Please* help me!'

'But why? Let them die quickly if you want to be kind to them. If we save their lives today, it'll be slow, certain death for us all tomorrow. There's just not enough to share. Be sensible, Johin, think of everyone, not just your own hare-brained notions.'

'That's just what I *am* doing. The River will take care of us,' she said.

'Oh, the River. You don't believe in all *that*, do you?'

Johin stamped her foot in frustration. 'You *saw* what happened today.'

'But that was some kind of illusion; a trick.'

'You ask your precious Chief whether it's an illusion!' she retorted. 'Anyway, when you last checked the pool, how full was it?'

'Almost dry, and very muddy.'

'And today, after I had taken some to save the life of one of the Sand people?'

Collim hesitated. 'It was very nearly full, the water was clear... and it looked very good.'

'Are you thirsty?'

'I'm always thirsty.'

'Have some.'

'Oh no, I'm not falling for tricks and potions. I've got work to do!' He stood up slowly and re-tied his white headband around his long hair.

Johin was persistent. 'It's quite safe, I am giving it to you. But don't take much, there are those whose need is greater than yours.'

Collim looked at her thin, earnest face. It was dusty and tired. He had always liked Johin, even though she was a little wild.

'Just to please you,' he said, taking one careful drink.

Suddenly he looked surprised and pleased, like someone who has just had an exciting idea. Then without another word he picked up two of the filled jars, and, with a spring in his step, hurried on up the rocks after Johin.

As they reached the camp of the Sand people, they heard dirge-like singing. One of the children was very near death. At the sight of two Mud people, the Sand people withdrew in silence, and looked on, terrified, as Collim and Johin went up to the dying babies under the trees.

Without hesitating, Johin repeated the slow operation of the night before. Using a piece of her own tunic, she squeezed drops of water between the babies' parched lips.

Collim looked around, stunned. Was *this* the 'enemy'? For the first time in his life he wanted to cry for someone other than himself. He looked at the dirty, swollen, fly-blown baby at his feet. He sat down and lifted the almost weightless child on to his lap. Without a word he copied Johin, tore a strip off the end of his headband, and started to squeeze precious drops of life-saving water into the baby's mouth.

Hour after tedious hour went by. Eventually the children began to breathe more freely, and a little colour came to their cheeks.

Johin dampened her own headband and washed the

dull red dust from the children's eyes and faces.

All the time, the Sand people stood back warily, scarcely able to believe their eyes. Here were two of the fierce Mud people giving precious water to Sand children!

Suddenly Johin sat back on her heels. 'Oh, I forgot! Manny! Leave the rest of the water there, Collim. Just bring that glass bottle. I must go to someone else.'

Collim followed, flushed with excitement.

Breathless, Johin ran up the barren hillside and flung herself into the cave entrance shouting, 'Manny! Manny! Are you all right? I'm coming!'

But the cave was empty.

3
Brilliance

A fire had been lit. A round, flat, wild grain loaf lay on a hot stone next to the embers.

'Welcome,' said a voice behind them.

It was Manny, but a very different sort of Manny. Although he *looked* just as he had before, something had changed. Here was the same dusty, scrawny Sand boy, with almost no hair and a threadbare kilt, yet he was somehow much more real and vivid than anyone Johin had ever seen before. Standing there, grinning from ear to ear, he seemed almost to burn with life.

'I thought you were nearly dead!' gasped Johin in amazement, almost dropping the bottle.

Manny ignored her surprise. 'Who's this?' he asked, holding his hand out to Collim.

Johin swallowed hard. 'This is Collim, he's my cousin. I know he's a Water Guard, but he's all right really ... and Collim, this is Manny ... he's ... he's ...' Johin hesitated. She realized she knew nothing about Manny at all. 'Well, if it hadn't been for Manny, I would never have found out about the pool,' she said.

Manny bowed slightly to Collim. 'Come and eat,' he said, 'You've earned it. There's enough for everyone, even Nuffle.' He lifted the little white ball of fur from Johin's shoulder, and set him on a large stone which had obviously been used for grinding the wild grains.

The little mouse was in heaven. He curled his long pink

tail around himself, and set to feasting on the tiny seeds left amongst the chaff.

Collim tucked into the chewy fresh bread. He and Nuffle were much alike. Good food and a comfortable corner came before any other considerations.

Johin crouched on a rock, staring suspiciously at Manny all the time. 'You were scarcely alive when I left you,' she said accusingly.

Manny grinned even more widely. He took a good mouthful of bread and sucked hard at the honey which he had used to bind the flour. Without finishing his mouthful, he explained. 'I come from the River ... The Lightwater is *my* River. The Pool is a part of the River. When the water thrives, so do I.'

'But the River is dying!' protested Johin.

'So am I,' he said thoughtfully. 'That's why I'm here.' Then he grinned again ... 'But for now, the Pool is filling, so we're having a party!' Manny produced two earthenware beakers and filled them with water from the bottle. 'Your ancestors left very useful things in these caves,' he said. 'Now, let us propose a toast ... to the River and to new beginnings!'

Collim raised his beaker heartily. 'If this is the beginning, I'm with it all the way. I've never tasted anything so good. But,' he hesitated suspiciously, 'seeing as you know so much, what *is* happening, with the Pool and everything ...? You see ...'

Manny laughed. 'Oh yes, the Chief Water Guard. He does make a splendid crocodile, but I'm afraid it will wear off in time. You see, the Pool *is* the Pool of Making. Its mud was used to make your race. While I am here, the Making within the Pool is so strong that it shows what people are really like inside. People who just help themselves will turn into what they most resemble ... but whoever is really in need or who takes the water to share, will remain human.'

Manny picked up little Nuffle and held him right in front of his face. Nuffle twitched his tiny white whiskers and held his huge pink ears erect. 'You, for example, my fine fellow, would make an excellent prince, don't you think? But your whiskers would have to be silver rather than white; that's a sign of wisdom, you know. I'm sure you're a very wise mouse!'

Collim felt a funny chill. How did this strange boy *know* about the Chief becoming a crocodile? Something about him prevented Collim from asking. He shrugged and smiled to himself as he drank again from the beaker. *He* had not changed into anything peculiar, and the Chief had only got what he deserved, after all.

Although Collim had said nothing, Manny looked at him sharply. 'Don't be too smug, Collim. Only this morning you were scheming how to get Sergeant Koos away from the water so you could have a good drink yourself.'

Manny hesitated and then with a glint in his eye he added, 'You would have made a marvellous monkey ... or perhaps being a donkey would have taught you how to become useful!' he added mischievously. 'And as for big black cats, Johin, you saw only what was within yourself.'

Collim hung his head, and concentrated on eating. Johin just looked stunned. She was not sure she liked this strange Sand boy who knew so much.

'Now listen, Johin,' said Manny. 'Time is very short, and I need your help. Go and tell everyone in your town that the Pool will only stay full if they share the water. Years and years of excluding the Sand people, selfishly helping yourselves to the River, then dumping all your rotting, poisonous rubbish in it, has reduced it to nothing. Even the source is clogged and choked.

'That's why I'm here—to Unmake the damage. And it

will have to be done very soon. The River is almost dead.'
Manny shook his head sadly. 'Your people think they *own*
the River, and that they are "special". But that's just not
true. You and the Sand people and every other being on
this planet were made by the Light within the River. You
were meant to share the River's life with each other. Your
very existence is a gift. The water is a gift, and you are
killing it.'

'But *I* can't tell the elders and everyone *that*,' protested
Johin. 'They'll laugh at me.'

'Does that matter?' asked Manny, giving her the sort of
look that made her feel ashamed.

'Anyway, why me?' she asked, horrified.

'Why *not* you? You have drunk from the Pool of
Making—the Lightwater will flow through you. Listen
to the River.'

Johin could think of no reply.

'Now, I have something very important to show you.'
Manny went into the dark recesses of the cave and
returned with a shallow earthenware bowl. It was
decorated with blue waves shining against the warm,
dull red of the clay.

He held it admiringly. 'Your ancestors were great
craftsmen.'

Crouching at the entrance to the cave, Manny filled
the bowl to the brim with fresh water from the never-
emptying glass bottle. He set the bowl on a rock, where
the evening sunlight poured in and struck the gleaming
water.

Kneeling down so that his eyes were level with the
brim, Manny joined his fingers and thumbs to made a
small round shape within his hands. Slowly he dipped
his hands into the bowl and scooped up a perfect
window of the water. He held it up carefully so it
caught the light, with a thousand dazzling rays thrown

into a glorious spectrum across the cave.

In the centre was a Face. At first it looked tiny, bright, and very beautiful, but it gave Johin a strange feeling. She did not like it.

As they looked, the Face grew bigger and more menacing, Manny lowered his hands, but the Face stayed. It had taken on a life of its own. He was strong. He was pressing, searching, hunting and tearing into every corner of the cave. At last his dreadful burning eyes rested on Manny. Johin and Collim were too terrified to breathe. Manny did not flinch. He stood up and looked straight at the apparition.

'Ah, I've been expecting you,' said the Face, leering at Manny as if he were about to devour him. 'What took you so long? Weren't you hungry and thirsty enough? I'll make it hotter if you like. Or has your precious River shielded you? You must be careful, you know. The agreement was that you would become just the same as the weakling humans.'

'You know I haven't cheated!' said Manny calmly. 'I fasted until someone brought me food and water of their own free will.'

'You're using plenty of your magic now, I see,' retorted the Face.

'Not for my own ends,' said Manny firmly.

The Face nodded at the bowl of water. 'If you did *that* trick in the valley, you'd soon have a good following. They like water-makers down there.'

Manny was angry. 'That is not the way of the River! My friends will learn to belong to the Lightwater because they want to, not because of magic tricks.'

'You know nothing about people!' sneered the Face, 'But *I*, on the other hand, know a great deal. All you need to do is to wave your hand over that precious River of yours and it would flood to fill the whole valley ... it'd drown the lot of them, then you'd have no more problems with stupid people ruining your precious Planet!' The Face began to laugh and swell until his menacing presence filled the whole cave entrance. A choking, rotting smell befouled the air.

'No!' shouted Manny. 'No! That is not the way! That will solve nothing!'

The Face grew and billowed. The same terrible sense of fear that had been around the valley for so long was now suddenly real and focussed. Here was its essence. Slowly, but firmly, like a great burning hand, the burgeoning evil pressed Johin and Collim down … down … on to their knees, squeezing the air and the life out of them. The weight was unbearable. At the same time the smell became an overpowering stench. Johin and Collim could hardly breathe. They coughed, straining their lungs for good air. Tears streamed from their stinging, swollen eyes.

Manny alone seemed almost unaffected. He stood firm, looking calmly into the eyes of the terrible Face, matching gaze for gaze.

Suddenly, Johin managed to struggle to her feet. She found herself shouting and flailing at the hideous form. She *had* to make the Face go away before he suffocated them all!

The Face looked at her for the first time. His evil eyes flickered. He raised a long golden eyebrow. 'You have the Mark, but it is not foolproof,' he sneered. 'One day I will absorb you too, and as for your pathetic friend over there, I can't imagine what he thinks he's up to with that toy!'

Collim was flattened against the cave wall. He was sweating in terror, his arms were shaking, and his eyes bulging, but somehow he was managing to aim his gun between the apparition's eyes.

The Face laughed again. It was the sound of an

insatiable thirst for death. 'Fire at me and you destroy yourself! Your puny weapons are nothing!' and with that the gun became a puddle of molten metal between Collim's feet.

Manny leapt forward. 'That's not fair, he doesn't know what's going on!'

'Who said anything about playing fair, my little man?' spat the Face. But with that, the last rays of light left the cave and the colours faded. So did the vision.

There was a long unbreathing silence as the air cleared.

'Who, or what, was that?' stammered Johin.

'His name is Brilliance. Who he was and is—well, that's a long story. *He* is the Enemy.'

'You said the Enemy was within our people,' replied Johin.

'He is, but that is what he looks like. He lives within people just as the River can.'

Collim was confused, and very frightened. 'But that face came out of the water of the Pool of Making, so he must be in that too ... is *he* really the Light of the River?'

'No, but he'd like to think so,' said Manny sadly. 'The Pool's water shows the true nature of things. My little window enabled us to look *through* the water and see the true nature of what is all around us. It is his effect on your people which is destroying so much. It is his work I am here to Unmake.

'The words of Unmaking will be terrible, but they must be said. Hundreds of years of misuse and pollution have poisoned the whole Planet. None of the Planet's people have cared about life, only about their own greed and cleverness, inspired by Brilliance.

'All around us, death and hopelessness are closing in. First, the land suffered, then the water, and now, the Lightwater itself. The riverbed is filled with rubbish, and even the source has become blocked. Deep beneath the surface, the water lies in dark underground lakes, poisoned and dying for want of light and release. This is what is causing the earthquakes and the drought. Nothing can live much longer.

'The water must be released, the poison and rubbish must be *Un*made. You saw how the water from the Pool of Making turned *people* into what they really were? In the same way it can restore all the shameful spoil of centuries to metals, minerals, and honest wood. *That* will be the Unmaking. It will mean everything can start again. If the source of the Lightwater can be freed, then there will be hope.'

'But won't people just do the same next time?' asked Johin.

'Yes. That is the effect of Brilliance. He has grown *inside* people like strands of fungus invading a rotting tree. He too must be Unmade, but that will be more difficult.'

Manny was silent for a while, then he looked at Collim.

'Now, Collim, you have seen the enemy in his own true nature, and you know why I am here. Will you, like Johin, take the Mark of the River? If you let it, it will protect you from evil, but it will also commit you to much danger ahead.'

Collim nodded dumbly. He was totally confused, but somehow he knew it was the only thing he *could* do. It was what he needed, and what he wanted. Manny took water from the Pool of Making, and in the dust on Collim's forehead, he traced the Mark of the Lightwater.

As Johin had done, he shivered, but he was glad.

The light was fading, but they could still see the strange boy's face, at the same time laughing and serious. Neither Johin nor Collim wanted to move.

'You must go back now,' said Manny. 'You are needed.'

4
The Fox and the Goose

Reluctantly, Johin and Collim obeyed, walking in stunned silence down to the Pool of Making. They felt dizzy with the day's events.

Johin wanted to be with Manny. He was more exciting than her old games. A sense of imminent danger and adventure hung about him. She wanted to go with him to this 'source', whatever it was.

Collim, on the other hand, was worried. Things had been fine when he was the big, tough Water Guard. He took no nonsense from anyone. What he said, went. Now, suddenly, he had discovered that someone else was stronger than he was—a skinny Sand boy with a mischievous smile, a couple of years younger than himself.

The Mark that Manny had made burned into his forehead. The memory of a dying baby in his arms burned into his mind. He wiped a tear away on the back of his hand. 'Mustn't waste water,' he mumbled.

As they approached the Pool, they heard what sounded like a cattle market in full swing. The place was alive with animals and beasts of every description, screaming and arguing in their own peculiar way. Most of them had linen tunics and kilts draped around their necks. All of them looked silly.

Johin and Collim laughed until they ached.

The crocodile was swimming round and round the

Pool, whipping water and mud into a foam with his thrashing tail.

There was a small flock of geese. Collim suspected they had been a crowd of annoying townswomen who usually did nothing but hiss and gossip about everyone and everything. Bowing and spitting, they glared and scorned all around them. They did not realize their own transformation, and were thoroughly enjoying being vicious about how silly everyone *else* looked.

A fat, fine boa constrictor was, Collim guessed, one of the town elders who was known for exacting taxes and water tolls to the last penny. Johin giggled. 'At least we can see him for what he is now.' The python obviously had ideas about lunching on a small flabby pair of pot-bellied pigs, still wearing their elders' shawls as they squelched heavily in the slippery delight of the mud.

Collim took the snake and wrapped it in a knot around a large rock. Coal-black eyes glowered at Collim. 'Stay there and be good,' Collim warned.

But Collim and Johin suddenly stopped laughing. Something terrible had happened. The Pool was almost empty again.

'What are we going to *do?* whispered Collim. 'This is awful!'

'I think I know,' said Johin. Can you make them sit down and shut up?'

With great difficulty, and a lot of chasing round and round the Pool, they managed to get the creatures sitting or lying quietly. Johin did her best to explain everything Manny had told them.

She stood on a rock and looked round at the crowd of animals. 'The Sand boy says you will become human again,' she said. 'But if any of us is going to survive, we must first restore the Pool of Making. You aren't going to like doing this, but the only way to fill the Pool is to help the Sand people. It's just the way the magic works.

'The Sand people aren't our enemies. They are just hungry and weak. Collim will show you where their camp is. You donkeys and ponies, go with him and bring the weaker ones to the Pool. You must help them to make camp here.'

Then with a wild guess she added, 'if you don't help, then every time you drink, you will become more stuck in your animal forms. The more you help and share, the more quickly you will return to normal, and the Pool will fill.'

She could sense the animals were furious, but they were unable to protest.

Collim pulled John to one side. 'You can't do that!' he said in horror. 'It's just not done ... it's degrading, and well, wrong! Mud people *never* help Sand people. All this drought is all their fault anyway! Everybody knows that!'

John swung round, furious. 'Have you forgotten those babies already? Have you forgotten the way the Pool filled this morning? How can you be so *stupid*, Collim? I'll do it alone if I have to. Go home and sulk if you like, but don't stop me!'

Collim sat in a confused, miserable heap, his head in his hands, unable to decide what to do.

John shrugged and took charge of the donkeys herself, leading them up towards the Sand people's camp. About halfway there, she met Manny, tenderly carrying two of the weakest children. With the help of the beasts of burden, the Sand people's meagre camp was packed, and thirty-one exhausted people were taken to the water's edge.

All night Collim dreamed he was a donkey. At dawn, he sullenly gathered all the digging and burrowing animals to clear and flatten the stony ground into a level campsite.

As they worked, the Pool filled, clear and clean.

Where water spilled on the ground, new, green growth sprang up. Johin had never seen more than a few stringy blades of grass before, but this was thick, dark and luxurious. It lay cool and soft beneath her toes. She watched some of the animals feasting on it, and tried a few blades herself. The sweetness was delicious, but it was too chewy to eat. Nuffle, who was keeping well out of the python's way, made a neat nest of the grass in Johin's pocket. He thought it was wonderful.

Manny worked alongside the stronger Sand people and the burrowing animals to irrigate and plant a small piece of land alongside the Pool. Almost overnight, a few basic crops began to thrive.

The Sand people regained their strength, and the Mud people dug a fresh channel to bring water from the Pool nearer to the town. Everyone was content.

Manny did his share of the work, digging and carrying, and helping to build shelters. He draped his kilt like a shawl over his head, against the raging heat of the sun. He was so thin, his old shorts had to be held up with several twists of twine.

Johin was worried. He looked so ordinary. Was that vision in the cave anything but heat-stroke? Collim wouldn't talk about it.

In the evenings, Manny would sit on the soft grass around the Pool. Hugging his kilt around his shoulders against the chill air, he sang and talked to anyone who was there.

On the third night, he sang the Song of the Making. Johin vaguely knew the story, but she had never heard it quite like this before.

At first, it sounded just like a small, soothing wind, creeping over the grass, then notes, sounds and words became clear. The children stopped squealing, the women ceased gossiping, and the men stood silent and awe-struck.

For the first time in living memory, Mud people and Sand people sat down together.

> Before time began
>> there was a great waiting
>>> the nothingness of space.
>
> The Maker breathed,
>> and the Light was born
>> sharper than a sliver of glass,
>> singing the highest, clearest note ever heard.
>
> Slowly the Light unfolded
>> into a million colours
>> bursting with music and life.
>
> Shattering, flowing, streaming
>> until the vast void became full of Lightwater.
>> Behold! Now they are one,
>> now they are together.
>
> See where the water withdraws
>> leaving moist, warm patches of earth
>> smelling rich and heady—
>> an earth wine.
>
> Deep in the water,
>> the lights draw together
>> into minute globes of fire,
>> trembling and spinning,
>> growing and swelling,
>> bursting from the depths
>> with bangs and crackles and firework bursts.
>
> But instead of cold fading cinders,
>> they laughingly explode into space.
>> See! Watch! The nothingness is no more,
>> it is night, and here
>> are stars and moons and suns.

Scarcely a week had passed, and the town of Ardigham was already different. It was alive and bustling.

The animals had mostly regained their human shapes, but the Chief's nose was rather longer than before. 'It's a little memento,' chuckled Manny.

Wherever Manny and Johin went, there was always a crowd. Johin loved being the friend of Manny the water-maker. She was respected and listened to. She liked being important.

Everything seemed to be going so well. The Pool was full, crops were growing, and people were making friends.

On the seventh night, Manny sat to sing at the Pool again, but this Song was one of sorrow and aching.

> *See the great Lightwater,*
> *flowing fast and free,*
> *commanding and singing as it goes.*
> *Out of its depths crawl creatures*
> *of every imaginable kind,*
> *and where it waters,*
> *green growth swathes the ground.*
> *Here and there, the River has drawn aside*
> *and made small, still pools.*
> *Here, Light gazes at its own reflection*
> *and smiles.*
> *In the depths, the rich red mud*
> *and the pale yellow sands*
> *stir, and gaze back at the Light.*
> *The River has given birth . . .*

As Manny sang, Johin lay back on the cool ground. She could see the song's story unfolding inside her head like a vivid dream.

She saw how the Light was not the only being that had

watched the Planet take shape. Another being, very bright to look at, but very evil, sheltered in the shadows behind the moon, nursing a deadly jealousy of all that was new and clean and happy.

Johin saw how he waited for endless years, simmering hatred as the people of the Mud became strong and skilled. Then she saw how with bitterness he turned his gaze to the pale people of the Sand. They had Light in their eyes as they sang wisdom and understanding.

She shuddered as she saw how he despised the people for their contentment as they lived together on the banks of the Lightwater. As Manny's song unfolded, Johin wondered at the calm peace of all she saw. Life was so steady and good.

At sunset, when their work was done, the people would gather and listen to the slow, deep speech of the River before going to their dwellings. The song told how the Light commanded the people never to be outside at night, when he was not there to guard them.

Horrified, Johin suddenly saw the bright figure was there too, dressed as a hard-eyed traveller. She watched him slip between the people and whisper, 'Why are you forbidden to go out at night?' Some told him it was because huge, flesh-devouring monsters roamed. Others thought if they couldn't see where they were going, they might fall down a deep pit and be killed. All agreed it was a command of love.

She watched as, with a sly smile, the strange traveller said: 'Perhaps there are great treasures to be gathered at night. I myself have seen the River full of silver and diamonds when the sun is gone. I think the Light is jealous, and doesn't want you to find them.'

Johin could see the shock on the listeners' faces. 'The Light would never be like that!' they cried.

'Wouldn't he?' wheedled the stranger. 'Let us go out

together tonight, and we shall see.'

The song told how the stranger showed them how to make a torch, an imitation light, so the people could see in the dark . . .

Something inside Johin made her want to shout out to them to stop, but she knew in her heart of hearts that she too wanted to see the River full of diamonds.

She could hear Manny's strong, clear voice, heavy with great depths of sorrow, telling how the people hesitated, and the strange traveller jeered at them for being scared of the dark, and unworthy of such adventure.

'So they stepped out into the night,' he intoned, 'and they found . . .'

'That they could see where they were going,' laughed a loud voice from the back of the crowd.

Johin jerked back to reality.

The Chief was stroking his long nose and grinning.

'That's right,' said Manny. 'It was then that people started to work long hours by their lights, inventing, making and throwing away. They ignored the Light which came to help them work, and went to give them rest. People suffered. The Planet became littered and poisoned with useless things: made for no good reason, then thrown away.

'That was the beginning of all this drought and destruction.'

'But it's all over now, isn't it?' asked one of the Sand people, pointing to the Pool.

Manny shook his head sadly. 'No, this is just a reprieve, a beginning of the Unmaking of the evil you have harboured all these years.'

The people looked embarrassed, and pulled away from Manny. 'We haven't done anything!' they muttered. 'It was the Sand people,' moaned the Mud people. 'It was the

Mud people,' complained the Sand people. Everyone went to bed cross.

No one liked Manny's miserable song. They only wanted him to keep the Pool full. Ardigham had water and food. What else mattered?

As the day faded, Manny stayed by the Pool. Johin and Collim sat with him for a while, but Manny wasn't in the mood for talking. He was hunched and turned in on himself. Collim, who preferred jovial company, soon left.

Johin tried sitting quietly next to him. At last she could stay silent no longer.

'Manny, what *are* you doing?'

'Listening.'

Johin was silent, but could only hear the sound of the wind in the leaves and the new grass, and an occasional strange, deep rumbling. There was nothing worth staying up all night for.

'What are you listening *to?*' she asked, bemused.

'I'm listening to the River,' he answered quietly, without moving.

'But that's way below in the canyon,' she argued. 'You can't possibly hear it up here.'

'I'm listening to the River within,' he replied, in his quiet, definite voice. But he would not explain. 'Why don't you sit with me and listen too?' he suggested.

She found that a frightening idea, and made an excuse to go.

The next day, the Mayor of Hogendam arrived on an official visit. His town lay next to the High Dam in the Hogendam Gap. The Water Guards and the Drought Council were based there. Some thought the Mayor had more power than the president, but they never said it out loud.

The Mayor of Ardigham had forgotten all about the

Hogendam delegation. He had been sitting contentedly in the sunshine, perched on a rock, bathing his feet at the edge of the Pool, his grandchildren splashing him all over.

The delegation found the town of Ardigham deserted, with the happy sounds of holiday fun drifting up from below. The visiting Mayor walked quietly down to the Pool. In silence, he climbed a lush grassy knoll overlooking the scene.

Without moving, he stood there, staring. His hatred and envy, as thick as a heavy fog, crept invisibly over the happy crowd, clamping and clutching at the hearts and throats of everyone there.

Nobody moved.

In the stifling silence, only one voice could be heard. It was Manny singing softly. It was an old song about a fox who was jealous of the goose and her small handful of corn.

When he finished singing, Manny stood up and bowed formally. 'Good evening, Mr Mayor,' he said. 'Welcome to Ardigham.'

The following day, the two mayors settled to their business. But Manny disappeared.

The first day, no one noticed. The Hogendam delegation caused such a stir in the town, no one gave a thought to Manny.

The second day, Johin and Collim searched long and hard for him.

The third day, the Mayor of Hogendam returned home.

At last people realized that Manny was not around. There was gossip and unrest. The people started arguing, and the elders talked about how this young boy had got the town into trouble with the Mayor of Hogendam, and then run away.

'We're better off without his sort,' said the elders. 'You can't trust these good-for-nothing Sand people to get on with a job. They are all talk and sing-song, then off they slope as soon as there's trouble!'

Johin was scared. Whenever she tried to defend Manny, they laughed at her and called her 'a silly child who doesn't understand these things'.

She was told to stay at home and out of mischief. Collim was put on 'other duties', well away from the Pool of Making.

Johin watched helplessly as the Sand people were given longer and harder work, while the Mud people took long, cool siestas in the shade of the tall young trees which had sprung up almost overnight around the Pool. 'After all,' said the elders, 'the Sand people were made from the desert sands, they are *designed* for this sort of work in these conditions. It would be cruel to keep them from it, just as it would be cruel to make *us* do work for which *we* are unfit . . .'

Johin's anger burned hot and furious, but without Manny, she was ignored.

One night, when all was quiet, she crept out into the still darkness. Where could Manny be? Collim assured her he had looked everywhere. The unaccustomed feel of cool grass beneath her feet was welcoming. She found a pleasant outcrop of rock which overlooked the valley. In the starlight she could see, far below, the thin silver ribbon of what remained of the River. She could just about hear it, too.

'Listen to the River, you will know what to do when the time comes.' That was what Manny had said to her the first day they'd met. It was so clear in her head, she would have thought he was standing next to her saying it.

She strained her ears as hard as she could. The minute

sound of rushing water, far below, almost mocked her. 'How can the stupid River tell me anything!' she sobbed, 'I need *Manny*!'

'Listen to the River; it is within you,' came the voice again. '*Listen!*'

'That's no good... I need Manny, not voices and dreams. You don't understand, everything's going wrong!' She had no idea to whom she was talking. It just all came out.

'Listen!' came the voice again. 'You're not *listening.*' The voice was so real this time that Johin jumped, and looked around.

Manny was sitting on the grass next to her, hugging his thin knees under his chin as he always did. She went cold all over. He had not been there when she had sat down. She had not heard him approach. She had not *felt* anyone there, until that moment.

He gave her his hand. In the starlight she could see he was smiling. 'I've missed you,' he said simply.

'Manny! Where have you been? Everyone is saying you ran away because you were scared of the Mayor of Hogendam. I just said you were busy. I couldn't believe you were scared!'

'No, I wasn't scared. I was listening. Like you should have been doing. The time has come for us to leave. But tonight, you must go home. You need some sleep. We have a long journey ahead of us.

'When we go, there won't be time to stop for good-byes. Follow me immediately, for your life, in fact everyone's lives, will be in great danger. We must go to the River's source. It's the only hope. There won't be a moment to lose.'

And with that Manny was gone. There was no one holding Johin's hand. She was completely alone on the hillside and very tired.

Silently she walked back home and crept back into bed. 'Was that listening, or was he really there?' she wondered vaguely, as she drifted off to sleep, her hand curled around Nuffle.

All across the dry hills and parched valleys, a low rumble disturbed the night. Stones and boulders were dislodged, and the air hung hot and languid.

Alone, Manny lay by the Pool, with his hands pressed to his sides in pain.

5

A Disastrous Escape

The row that followed the Hogendam delegation's visit was dreadful.

Ardigham was in ferment. The Mayor, the elders and the Water Guards all blamed each other. However it had happened, Sand people should *never* have been allowed near the town.

The Mayor of Hogendam had promised to send Drought Council Inspectors to Ardigham. They would doubtless withdraw all privileges and impose stiff penalties, unless the Council's rules were returned to immediately.

He had lectured the Ardigham elders on the serious-ness of the water situation. He insisted that the Sand people must be returned to their traditional lands. Their presence in Ardigham could not be tolerated. He said that in no way could Sand people *ever* be considered as genuinely in need. They had their own very effective ways of finding water. They were lazy, that was all.

Above all, the Mayor of Hogendam insisted, that trouble-maker Manny must be got rid of, and quickly.

The Chief could see that something would have to happen. He persuaded the Mayor and the elders to let *him* handle the whole affair.

He stroked his long nose, and thought.

While Manny was with the Sand people, the Chief knew he could do nothing, but when the boy was in the town, there was a chance. He watched, and waited, and calculated. He told the Mayor of Ardigham his plan. Then he began to get nervous. Never before had he carried out an arrest quite like this one.

Then came the order to move in.

The night was still, but very dark. A high dust storm obliterated the stars. A strange eerie rumbling echoed in the hills, but everything else was silent. Collim was sent for.

He found the Chief sitting at his desk looking very straight-backed and stern. On the desk were two guns and a green leather bag, about the size of a man's fist. The Chief seemed nervous.

'We are to arrest Manny tonight,' he said flatly. He was not looking at Collim.

'I can't do that!' protested Collim, ' . . . nor can you!'

He knew he was risking court-martial by challenging his superior, but he had suspected for some time that the Chief was at least sympathetic to Manny.

Collim tried to catch the Chief's gaze, but he kept looking away.

'You can choose,' said the Chief. 'You can take a gun and come with me to arrest the boy in the ordinary way . . .'

The Chief fell silent. He seemed to be waiting for an answer.

Collim said nothing for a long time, then taking a deep breath he decided to risk everything: 'Or?' he asked.

'Or you can take this,' the Chief said, pushing a long skein of fine rope on to the table. It was like silk, but Collim knew it would easily take the weight of a man.

The Chief spoke very quietly, as if he was afraid of being overheard. 'I have told the Mayor the arrest will be in one hour. Manny is at Johin's house. You must go now, so there is time for him to get a head start.

52

'In case the house is being watched, slip round to the back window and get him out that way. Take him well away from the road. Try and get him to that long ledge halfway down the canyon—you know the one. Then he must run. I can't protect him. I'll just tell the Mayor he fled before the arrest.' The Chief pushed the green leather bag across the desk. 'There's plenty of gold in there. It'll help the lad on his way a bit.'

At last the Chief met Collim's gaze. He looked gaunt, and as if he were pleading with Collim to help.

Without saying a word, Collim picked up the rope and the bag. It was a cold night, so he pulled a grey blanket around his shoulders and tucked the rope under its folds. Thankful for the cover of night, he ran as stealthily as he could to Johin's house.

Tapping lightly at the window, he called for Manny.

'Are they after me so soon?' said the boy. He looked pale and tired.

Johin was asleep. Her mother shook her firmly by the shoulder. 'Manny's going,' she said. 'You must go too.'

Johin sat up in amazement. 'You *want* me to go? But why? You always complain I'm never home!'

Her mother twisted her hands tightly. 'We don't *want* you to go, but things are too dangerous here. Just go for a while—a few days. When the fuss has died down, you can slip back, and no one will remember you were ever in trouble. It's because we love you. Can you see that?'

Johin looked questioningly at her father. 'Yes, I agree,' he said. 'We've talked about it a lot. I know Manny will look after you. But I wish you'd take Collim with you.'

'But I'll be all right with Manny!' she protested.

'No, I want *you* to look after Collim. He needs to be kept out of trouble too!'

Johin hesitated as the Sand boy climbed out of the window, clutching the old glass bottle. 'Manny wants me to go as far as the source of the River with him,' she said glumly. 'It could be a long time before I'm back . . . I'll miss you!' She could feel tears in her eyes, and her throat was tight. Suddenly she found she was hugging her parents. After all her dreams of adventure, she knew she really did not want to leave them.

Collim rattled at the window. 'Hurry up, Johin, we can't wait! Meet us by the broken part of the quay wall. We must move!'

Johin put on her sandals, and caught Nuffle. The unfortunate mouse was stuffed deep into her grass-lined pocket as she kissed her mother and father, and clambered across the window ledge.

Just as she landed softly in the dust outside the window, there was a splintering crash. A few well-aimed axe blows and the old door was reduced to a pile of sticks. Collim heard the distant noise, and guessed that the Mayor had decided to take no chances about whose side the Chief was on.

Johin slipped along a dark side street, running the opposite way from the route she guessed Manny and Collim would take. Quietly, she crept up behind the Water Guard Station, and down to the meeting place. There she crouched and waited.

Collim had taken Manny's hand and pulled him this way and that through the backstreets. He decided against trying to get out through the old stream conduit. There was a steep drop from the water outfall, and Collim was not sure of a good fastening for the rope. Up steps they ran, along rooftops and then down disused drains, running until they felt their lungs would burst.

Each way they went there were heavy footsteps and hard breathing just behind them. Collim was getting scared.

Suddenly the strange distant rumblings exploded into

ear-splitting crashings and grindings. The ground shifted, and they were thrown backwards. Manny did not get up. Frantically, Collim scooped him up and ran with him across the heaving ground. The earthquake stopped as suddenly as it had started.

In a final effort of will, Collim flung himself and his almost lifeless burden into a tiny crevice between a derelict house and a rock fall.

To Collim's relief, Manny seemed to recover himself fairly quickly. 'It's all right, Collim,' he whispered. 'I'm not hurt, it's just a pain that comes and goes.'

'Thank goodness,' said Collim. 'For a skinny lad you're quite a weight. I couldn't have carried you far. Now listen, we have got to get you away from here, quickly. Are you well enough to run?'

Manny swallowed hard and gritted his teeth. 'Yes, I'll have to be.'

Collim took Manny's hand firmly. 'Hold on to me, don't let go; in this dark you'll never find me again, and we're very near to the edge.'

Together they climbed up the rockfall. Collim was glad there was no moon, because from here they would have been silhouetted against the sky for all the town to see. Then came the difficult part, climbing down the other side.

'We must let go now, we'll need both hands here ... Can you see me?' whispered Collim hoarsely.

'No, but if you keep talking I can follow you by sound,' said Manny. Step by step they made their way down the rockface, Collim telling Manny every tiny move to make, and slowly they groped their way down.

From above, in the town, they could hear the hue and cry starting up again.

'Don't worry, we've led them a good chase,' he joked. 'Johin will be all right. She'll be waiting a little further along. I'll let you down, then I'll get her and she'll join you at the bottom.

Collim was so busy talking, he did not check his handholds. The earthquake had loosened familiar rocks, and he slipped.

There was a stifled gasp, a soft thump and silence.

'It's all right, I'm fine,' said Collim at last. 'Just bruises. But I've dropped the rope, and I can't see you.'

Manny started singing, one of the ancient songs of the Sand people. Following the sound, Collim groped his way over to Manny. They grasped each other's hands in the dark. They were both sweating and trembling. In Manny's hand lay the thin thread of the rope. How he had found it, Collim could not guess, but he could not stop to think about it.

'Have you ever done abseiling?' asked Collim hopefully.

'No. What's that?'

'Oh well, it's time for you to put every bit of trust you have in that River of yours,' said Collim dryly. 'It means going down a cliff backwards.' He showed Manny how to twist the rope around his waist and legs, so he could control descent with one hand.

'You're lucky to have a goat-hair kilt,' said Collim, 'you won't burn yourself. This fine rope cuts terribly.'

The sounds of shouting and running seemed to be getting closer, so with a friendly shove he launched Manny over the cliff edge, into the dark.

'You'll reach a ledge before the end of the rope. It's wide and firm. You'll know when you're there. Just untie yourself, and give me two tugs to let me know you're clear of the rope.

With a few scrapes and bleeding toes, Manny landed on the ledge.

'I'm on a shelf wider than I am,' he whispered up.

'Good, that's it. Turn to your left and the ledge will take you on a good path down to the River. You must keep walking upstream as long as you can. You must be well out of sight before dawn. Good luck, and may your River keep you safe. I hope we meet again.'

Just then they heard a barking above the sound of voices. Someone had brought a dog!

'Come down, Collim; you'll never escape if you stay where you are!' called Manny urgently.

Somehow, Collim felt that Manny knew what he was talking about. With a couple of movements he had twisted the rope around himself, secured the loose end around a rock, and had slipped down next to Manny. Blindly, they began to grope their way along the ledge.

Suddenly a loud and urgent wailing pierced the black night. It was almost above them.

'Maaaannyyy ... Maaaannyyyyy!'

Collim could feel Manny go rigid.

'It's Johin!' he said in a strained hush. 'Oh no, go back, Johin ... go *back!*'

They heard stones dislodge somewhere above them, a thin scream and something fell in the dark, dark night.

6
Manny's Song

'Which is the quickest way down?' demanded Manny urgently.

'In this dark it could take an hour or more to get to the bottom, and then we'd have to wait until dawn to find her.'

'And if it wasn't dark?'

'Well, if we had the moon and the rope, we could be down in a couple of minutes I guess... but what's the point? Johin's dead; she must be. You get away, and we'll get her body up when it's light.'

'You don't understand!' said Manny in a way that made him sound almost angry. But he was crying.

Then he lifted both his hands to the sky and sang something... it was not in the speech of the Sand people. It was a very cold sort of music, and it sounded like a demand. Then he blew gently, and high above, the dust clouds parted, and a full, bright moon shone almost as clear as midday.

Collim gasped: 'I don't believe this.'

While Collim stood open-mouthed, staring incredulously at the light-filled sky, Manny had run back up the ledge, and with one good flick, had pulled the rope loose from its moorings at the top. He coiled it neatly over his arm and shoulder as he ran. Breathless, he was standing next to Collim again. 'Fasten this for me, and show me how to do that abseiling again... Hurry!'

With shaking, sweaty palms, Collim did as he was told, and guided his friend over a precipice for the second time that night.

'Follow me down immediately. I'll need you,' ordered Manny. Collim was numb with shock and amazement, but he obeyed.

In the bright moonlight, Johin's long, thin body was easy to find. She was not alive; there was no way she could be. She was lying twisted and broken with one thin, dark red arm draped in the fast-flowing waters of the River. Her long straight hair was spread out around her. A warm trickle of blood seeped from the corner of her mouth.

Everywhere was noise. High above them the pursuers were shouting, and the dog was howling for its lost quarry. But greater than it all was the ceaseless rushing of the River.

Manny scooped up Johin's loose body, and, crying freely, he waded into the River. Holding her firmly, he dipped her deep into the water and sang again.

It was a slow, breathing sort of song, cool and rhythmical. It seemed to be almost one with the flow of the River. Then, without stopping his strange singing, Manny lifted her head up. He was choking with tears, but he did not stop his song for one instant. He stroked the blood- and water-soaked hair back from her face.

'Wake up, Johin,' he sang. 'Wake up'.

Nothing happened. She lay still.

Manny sang on.

Long moments passed, then Johin's eyes flickered and opened.

She groaned. 'Oh my head! I must have hit it. What happened? How did I get here?'

'You fell,' he said simply. 'But you're all right now. What happened?'

Johin stood shaking with cold, waist-deep in the River. 'I think it was the Mayor's dog. It's a horrid animal. It's never liked me. It came for me. I could see its bared teeth, even though it was pitch dark up there.'

Collim stood on the bank of the River in disbelief. As he took Johin's hand to help her out of the water, he felt the surge of life-magic that Manny had been pouring into her. It was so strong, it made him want to sing, if only he had known how.

This was something stronger than he had ever known. He wanted to hug it, but at the same time to run far, far away. He found he was crying.

He put his blanket around Johin's shoulders. She was shivering hard now, and the approaching grey dawn brought a fresh, cold wind.

'The townsfolk will be down soon for their morning water,' said Collim. 'You'd better get on your way.'

Manny looked up at the town. 'You're right. Are you ready, Johin? Are you coming, Collim?'

Collim, still feeling stunned and dazed from the night's events, shook his head. 'How can I? I've got work to do.'

Manny looked sad. 'As you will!' he said simply. 'But I'd be glad if you came.'

'Thanks. Later, perhaps.'

'Yes. Later,' said Manny.

Johin gave Collim a hug and returned his wet blanket. 'Take care, and look after Mum and Dad for me, will you?'

'Of course.'

'Send them my love, tell them everything's fine ... and ...' she hesitated, whispering, 'Collim ... what *did* happen just then?'

Collim smiled a little shyly and shrugged. 'I'll tell you when I've worked it out for myself.' He grinned and roughed her wet hair. 'Take care, Johin.'

With that he started to climb the steep path up to the

town. He was not sure where he was going, but he had vague thoughts of going home to tidy up before returning to the Guard Station for his duty list.

Johin ran on the spot to warm herself.

Suddenly she gasped. 'Nuffle! I hope he's all right!'

She pulled him out of her pocket, limp, wet, and cold. Her heart sank.

'May I see him?' asked Manny. The boy stroked Nuffle with one long, yellowish finger.

'He's fine,' he said.

7

Summons to Hogendam

Collim was cold, hungry, and miserable.

As he walked home, he could not shake the memory of Johin and Manny walking away together.

He shrugged and tried hard to pretend that he did not wish, even then, to drop everything and run after them. He pushed open the door of his bungalow. The dark heat hit him. He sank down on his bed and slept.

It was almost noon when Bram, one of the cadet Water Guards, knocked on the door. Collim did not answer. Bram pushed the door open. It squeaked badly, and a knife-like shaft of light sliced across the room. Collim grunted and sat up.

'Who's there?'

'Bram,' came the reply. 'The Chief wants you; full uniform in ten minutes.' Bram hesitated. 'If you ask me, you're for the high jump. There's an inspector there from Hogendam! He looks none too pleased, either.'

Collim blinked at the searing light. 'Fine!' he croaked. 'Tell him I'm coming.'

He staggered over to the water pot, took a drink and washed as best he could in the small ration allowed. He brushed and tied his headband. He had no clean uniform, but the one he had slept in was better than the one in a heap in the corner; both smelt and were dust-stained.

As he struggled with the knots in his sandal thongs, he began to wonder why the Chief had sent for him. The news of last night's bungled arrest could not have reached Hogendam yet. With no mishaps, it was a straight two-day march by road, or half a day by hoverbike (although that was only used for top priority business).

It did sound like trouble though. Perhaps his involvement with Manny had been reported . . . but the Chief had never said anything. Collim began to feel worried. Was it still too late to run after Manny and Johin? He wished more than ever that he had gone.

In the dark shadows he tried to trace the shape of Manny's Mark on his forehead. Manny had said something about 'protecting you from evil—if you let it'. He hoped Manny was right. News from Hogendam was bound to be bad.

Collim made his way through the town, trying to make himself feel brave and confident. Despite his broad shoulders and determined stride, he was scared. In the old days, he could have bullied his way through any situation. Since Manny had come, things had changed. He did not really know how to cope any more.

He had been to Hogendam a few times. He had done his basic training there, of course, they all did. Hours of exercises on the flat grey squares. Parades in the sun, and combat training in the bleak hills and stinking marshes, cowering from the vicious sandstorms that blew in from the desert.

A summons to Hogendam meant trouble.

Collim stepped over a pile of rubble where one of the town's older houses had collapsed in the previous night's earth tremor. It hadn't been bad, only a shiver, really, but some of the buildings were very weak.

The Water Guard Station in Ardigham was next to the fountain basin. It looked quite odd, a square concrete bungalow like all the other new buildings, but placed amid the crumbling grace and elegance of the old town. It was always a shock to see it.

Collim knocked at the door and went in. The visitor was a sight to behold. He wore the stiff dark blue belt with the burnished copper insignia of a Chief Inspector. His tunic was immaculately white, and his headband was neatly tied. He scowled at Collim. 'This is number 2461?' he asked, in horror.

'Yes,' said the Chief, a little hesitantly.

'He's a mess. Get him tidied up. Put a clean uniform on him!' he snapped.

The Chief rubbed his long nose nervously. 'None of us has a clean uniform, sir. There is a complete ban on washing clothes.'

'That doesn't apply to Water Guards, you fool!' the Inspector snapped. He was a small, lean man with a thin, twitching face.

'I wonder what Manny would turn *him* into?' Collim asked himself. 'A rat, I bet.' He tried not to smile.

'Well,' said the Inspector at last, 'I suppose you will have to do. Your Chief was told to nominate one of his staff to come to join the Inspectorate at Hogendam. It is a privilege accorded to each station from time to time. For some reason, he thinks you are the best candidate for the job. He says you are excellent at organizing people, and at keeping trouble at bay.

'Personally, I doubt it. Go and pack, and say whatever goodbyes you must. We leave on the hoverbike at three sharp this afternoon. That will be all.' The little man saluted, and strode out of the door, nose in the air and small black eyes glinting.

Suddenly he reappeared and scowled at the Chief.

'Where's that cadet of yours?' he called. 'I want a complete guided tour of all the town's water and food supplies.'

Bram scuttled up to him and saluted rather badly. 'This way, sir,' he said. 'I'll show you our Pool first, sir. I think you'll be impressed.'

Collim dashed to the door and called after Bram, 'Do allow the Chief Inspector to drink from the fountain first, won't you? I don't think he'll *like* the Pool water; that's only for the *ordinary* people, after all.'

Bram grinned and nodded. He could see it would be very funny, but also very embarrassing to have to return a small sharp-nosed creature to Hogendam, instead of a Chief Inspector!

Collim went inside and stood in front of the Chief, who was sorting papers on his desk without looking at him.

'What *is* all this?' he demanded.

The Chief still didn't look up. 'I'm sorry, Collim, I thought it would be for the best. I could see that sooner or later you were going to be for the high jump over Manny, so I recommended you for promotion, to get you out of the way.'

At last he looked up. 'I still think it might be a good idea. I'm sorry I didn't warn you. I didn't know you'd been accepted until the Inspector arrived first thing this morning. I told him you'd been on night duty, and I held off waking you. But I couldn't warn you.

'Meanwhile we have trouble. Last night's earth tremor has fractured the pipe to the pump. I don't know if the Inspector will get his drink there. Then the Sand people have all disappeared and, of course, so has Manny.' The Chief sat down, looking exasperated.

Collim nodded. 'I know Manny's gone—so has my cousin Johin. I don't know where. I don't think they'll be back for a long time. Anyway, I'd better go and get packed. Thanks for trying to help.'

As Collim turned to leave, the Chief asked: 'But what do I tell the Chief Inspector about the Pool and the crops and the irrigation and everything?'

Collim shrugged. 'Try the truth,' he said.

8
Capture!

Johin was dizzy.

She had never walked so far or so fast. The endless barren desert sand and the purple haze on the hills began to be frighteningly the same. She found she longed for the fresh greenness of her part of the valley. Manny rationed her strictly to two gulps from the precious water bottle every hour.

Soon after noon, Johin staggered and lay still on the ground. 'What's the hurry? Where are we going anyway? I don't care if a bear is after me, I'm staying here for a rest. I've got to!'

'Well, at least get into the shade,' said Manny as he hooked his arm under her shoulder, and heaved her up. 'I'm sorry if I've been going too fast. I wanted to get as far as possible before we really stopped.'

'Who'd bother about a couple of kids going off for a day or two?'

'I can think of several people who would rather I stayed where they could see me,' he said ruefully. 'Let's rest in the shade of those rocks. Are you thirsty?'

'That's a stupid question,' she said crossly as she took a good swig from the bottle. 'Does this thing never empty?' She shook the bottle and it sloshed satisfyingly half full.

Manny shrugged. 'Does a River empty? We have all we need while we need it. When we don't need it, or when the River wants us to find another part of the flood, then it will empty. Until then, we give thanks for what we have.' He closed his eyes and sang a few long, slow notes. Then he drank two long gulps, and curled up to sleep in the shade.

They heard the jingling of tiny brass bells on the camel straps first, then they saw the Wanderers, mounted on fifty or sixty heavily-laden camels. They were so colourful! Johin had never seen anything like it. Her own people were forbidden to use dyes, which needed a great deal of water. Everything they had at home was undyed and unbleached. Anything with colour was usually very old.

But these Wanderers wore long, loose robes woven in such rich, strong hues that Johin thought at first it must be the President, or visiting royalty. Next came the overpowering smells of exotic spices and camel dung. The myriads of tiny bells caught the mid-afternoon sun with dazzling stabs of light. Johin could not help staring, openmouthed.

Manny leapt to his feet and hailed them. 'We need a blanket!' he called up to the leader on his camel, craning his neck and shading his eyes. 'Do you have a good thick one to trade?'

The camel train halted, and two young men unrolled half a dozen blankets from a pack. Manny picked out a thick goat-hair rug. It was grey and very scratchy, but he insisted that Johin bought it.

'The nights are cold, and you are not used to sleeping rough,' he said. Johin had wanted a soft fluffy one which was dyed in purple and blue stripes. She had never owned anything so lovely, and she fingered it longingly, but the men wanted two gold rings for it. She only had one, and she did not want to part with that: it was her family's token. Everyone wore one; a token ring was almost as important as one's name among the Mud people.

'Without a blanket you will be cold and uncomfortable,' insisted Manny. 'Fifty token rings won't keep the night chill off you. Don't you remember how cold you were by the River this morning? Now look, the goat-hair one is better than the fluffy one; it will keep out the wind and the sand better. The one you like will become clogged and matted, and soon it will be no good at all.'

So the bargain was struck. Johin reluctantly surrendered her precious token ring to an old brown lady of mysterious ancestry. Her face was as wrinkled as a dried prune, and her piercing black eyes glinted as she took her payment. Johin found herself rather scared yet fascinated by this strange, pungently perfumed grandmother.

She watched the old lady climb delicately up on to the camel seat. Her loose blue robes fluttered gently around her as the camel rose to its feet with a huge dipping motion.

As the camels moved away, Manny noticed that one of the beasts was lame. That was serious. It meant the Wanderers could not travel far to trade. If a water hole was dry, there would be no way of getting everyone to the next watering place quickly, as the whole train must go at the speed of the lame camel. It could mean death.

'Will you give me a satchel of provisions if I cure your camel?' Manny called.

The camel train halted, and the leader, they called him their King, stopped and sniffed. He was a heavy-looking man with iron-grey hair and an orange robe. He scowled and grunted, and peered suspiciously down at Manny. '*Can* you?' he demanded. 'You're very young to claim such skills!'

'Is it a bargain?' Manny asked.

The man hesitated, then he grunted again. 'Yes, on one condition.'

'What's that?'

'You stay with us tonight. If you harm the camel, if it is

any worse by morning, then we will have the girl. She will fetch a good price at market.' Johin shuddered. She wasn't quite sure what they were talking about, but it felt horrid.

Manny nodded and lifted the camel's foot. It had a running wound. Thick, foul-smelling pus oozed on to Manny's hand.

'Give me clean rags,' he said.

The prune-faced grandmother made her camel sit. She rummaged in her basket and produced a handful of scraps.

Manny uncorked their precious bottle. He damped one or two of the rags and wiped the stinking pus from the camel's wound. He went to the beast's head, and placed a hand on its neck. Instead of spitting in Manny's eyes, as camels usually do with strangers, it just bowed its head and knelt.

'Give me a long needle, please, Grandmother,' said Manny to the old lady. She looked up at the Wanderer-King, who nodded. She fetched a thick, embroidered roll of cloth from her saddle bag, and drew out a long, curved carpet needle.

Speaking softly to the beast all the time, Manny dug at the wound until he pulled out a large black thorn. The stench from the pus was sickening, but Manny bathed the foot with a few more drops from the bottle, then bound it with the rest of the rags. The camel lowered its long grey neck, and slept.

The King was furious.

He sucked his lips between his teeth and stared viciously at Manny. 'You have killed a good beast with your magic. Your magic is a bad magic, and I will kill you!' Muttering oaths, the King swung down from his own beast and darted at Manny. Just then, the lame camel, wakened by the shouting, jerked its head up sharply, and spat a well-aimed mouthful of bile into the King's face.

'Let him sleep,' said Manny quietly. 'You will find him healed in the morning.'

The old man wiped the offensive spittle from his eyes with a sleeve. 'Huh! We shall see! You will stay here with us, just to be sure.' With that he gave orders for camp to be made where they were.

As it was still only mid-afternoon, the Wanderers' children were sent out to look for drought fruit and wild grains. A goat was killed and roasted, and flat, black bread was baked on hot stones around the fire. The Wanderers kept well away from Manny and John, but two strong men with cruel-looking curved knives in their hands were set to guard them.

They were a strange race. Even more despised than the Sand people, they were mostly the offspring of criminals, sent out into the desert as a punishment for their misdeeds. Those who survived banded into strong family groups and became good traders, who travelled extensively. They were a mixture of all races—the outcasts of every nation—but they were strong, with a fierce pride. In gorgeously-coloured flowing robes, with heavily embroidered shawls pulled over their heads, the Wanderers looked strange and magnificent on their high mounts.

No one feared them when they came into the towns. Part of their punishment was the curse of death on any who stayed in a town at night, and the magic was strong. Out in the open country, however, they ruled. An unwary traveller who met up with the wrong band stood little chance of escape.

One or two of the younger Wanderers came and pinched John's arm, and made her stand up and turn around a few times. They nodded and agreed that she would 'do'.

Manny and John were pushed into a small black goat-hair tent. Their feet were bound to the centre pole with dried gut. The knots were impossibly tight and could not be unpicked.

'Couldn't you sing one of your songs and undo the knots?' asked Johin.

'I could.'

'Well, what are you waiting for?'

'If they see us untied they will kill us first and ask questions afterwards.'

'But if we *don't* get untied we won't escape!' said Johin frantically.

'But if we do escape, we will have to spend the night on the run, and that will be both tiring and unpleasant. Let us sleep first, and then we will be strong enough to run in the morning.'

'We're not just going to *stay* here, and be killed in our sleep!' Johin was very frightened. She desperately wanted to run as far and as fast as she could. All night, if necessary. She had bloodthirsty Wanderers on one side, and on the other, a mad boy, who would not lift a finger to save himself.

Suddenly the tent flap opened, and a boy came in with roast goat meat and some black bread. Then the old grandmother who had given Manny the needle brought two small bowls of strong tea. She had Johin's blanket under her arm. She looked at them both and shook her head, clicking her tongue.

As soon as they had gone, Manny smiled reassuringly. 'The River cannot be bound. You'll see. We will be free in the morning, but first you need rest. They won't kill us tonight. The smell of blood would bring jackals into the camp, and that's the last thing they want. We are safe until morning, I promise you.'

'But my ankles hurt,' Johin moaned crossly, 'and I can't get comfortable. How can I get to sleep like this?'

71

Manny sighed and sat up. He reached out and touched the bindings. Johin could not tell whether they actually loosened, or if they just *felt* better. But she could lie still at last.

As night fell, there was silence in the camp. The Wanderers seemed to have gone to sleep.

Johin called out softly, 'Are you awake, Manny?'

'Yes.'

'I'm scared. Leaving home hasn't seemed real until now, it was a sort of a jaunt—a day's outing. But now ... I'm frightened.'

'Are you sorry you came?'

'No, but I still don't understand why we had to run away like that. What harm have we done anyone? You especially; you only ever tried to help!'

'Your people had everything they could want— plenty of water and a slave workforce. They want you and me out of the way because we make them feel guilty. They know it's wrong to treat the Sand people the way they do. They know they've helped to cause the Lightwater to fail. They want to get rid of us because they can't live *with* us. If we had stayed, we would have met with an unfortunate "accident". Anyway, we couldn't have stayed. We have work to do. We must reach the source quickly. Time is short.'

Johin shifted uncomfortably on the rocky sand. She could feel tears burning like pepper into her eyes. She could hear Nuffle scratching around in the dark for the remains of the supper. She was glad he was there, but that wasn't enough. Suddenly she could not help herself, and she burst into tears. 'I want my Mum!'

She sobbed loudly for a few minutes, then between the sniffs she tried to talk again. 'You know, Manny, it seems strange: Mum and Dad used to complain that they never saw me. Yet they *insisted* that I ran away with you. Just as I was begining to realize how much I loved them, I had to go. I only wish that Collim had come too.'

'Why?'

'I just feel he *ought* to be here, if you know what I mean ... But I still want my Mum, and Dad too. Will I ever see them again?'

'If all goes well,' said Manny thoughtfully. 'I hope so. Really I do.' Manny shuffled over to her, and squeezed her hand. 'I'm right next to you now. Does that feel better?'

'Yes', came Johin's voice in a choked sort of way. She sniffed back more tears and wiped her nose on the blanket.

She was quiet for a few minutes, then suddenly she blurted out, 'But *why*, Manny? What's it all for? Where *is* this "source" you keep talking about? What are we going to do when we get there?'

'The source of the Lightwater is deep below the hills, behind the great city, the other side of Hogendam. When we get there, we must free the River. For centuries the life waters of the Planet have been slowly clogged and poisoned. The Planet's peoples were brilliant. They could make anything. But as more and more wonderful things were made, the older makings were tossed aside to leave room for the new. No one cared about the poisonous waste, or the clogging rubbish. Now you are left with the ruin of the Planet. But still the peoples are selfish and cruel, and they are destroying what little is left. Soon there will be no water or life left at all. Everything will die.

'All this will have to be Unmade. It is a terrible magic, as strong and as deep as the Magic of Making. Once the life of the Planet is out of danger, I can tackle Brilliance, who has inspired all this. His Unmaking will be much more difficult and dangerous. His essence is deeply woven into people. He must be Unmade from the inside out.'

Johin thought for a minute. 'If *you* are . . . you know . . . from the River, why can't you just magic everything bad away? Why go through all this Unmaking? Why go around as a mere Sand boy, and a pretty pathetic specimen at that? Why didn't you come as the Planet President or something? Then you could *make* people change.'

'I can't just "magic" it as you say, because I am what you see, a Sand boy, so I've got to do things the human way. Anyway, *making* people change achieves nothing. They've got to *want* to be different.'

Johin was furious. 'Don't you *care?* There are thousands of people between here and Hogendam dying from thirst, poison and earthquake, and you're sitting here tied up in a tent! I don't believe a word of all you say about it being *your* River! If there really *was* a Light in the River, it wouldn't have *let* all this happen in the first place. If the River really *was* anything to do with you, you'd wave your hand and it would all be all right again!'

'Johin,' said Manny quietly, 'I'm doing it this way so that you can see that what I do is also possible for someone ordinary like you to do. If I were the President, or if I just "waved my hand" or used magic water from the Pool, it would be only a temporary measure—a patching-up job. It would do nothing about the invasion of Brilliance deep down within people.

'There can be no short cuts. It's like the camel's hoof: putting ointment on it might have helped to ease the pain, but the thorn had to be dug out to heal the wound properly, or the camel would have died. That's what I've got to do. Can you see?'

'Do you mean you're going to get a thorn out of the source of the River?'

'Sort of. Hundreds of years of very big and very evil thorns.'

'But why get *me* involved? I was quite happy at home... I'm only ordinary and *me*. You're from the River, or so you say. It's your job, but not mine! I was quite happy until you came along!'

Manny felt for her hand in the dark. 'I need you. I need a friend. I need lots of friends: people I can trust to carry on where I leave off, so all this will never happen again...' He hesitated a little. 'You're not really sorry you met me, are you?'

'No,' she sniffed. 'I'm glad, honestly. I feel as if things are going to be all right when you're around, but when I think about other things, things where you aren't, if you know what I mean, then I get scared.'

'Then don't think that way, think of everything as having me there in the middle, because that's the truest way of seeing things. Now sleep, Johin. You will need all your strength; we have a long way to go.' He put his skinny hand over her eyes, and she began to feel as if she was floating and drifting.

As sleep started to come, she heard a deep voice calling out to them: 'Don't try to escape; you are well guarded.'

'Wouldn't dream of it,' muttered Manny, and then there was silence.

9

The Flying Mouse

Johin snapped awake.

What was that rustling sound? There was definitely a scraping noise near her head. She opened her mouth to call Manny, and a thin, strong hand slapped a rag between her teeth.

'One sound from you, and we'll all be for the slave market,' whispered a small voice. 'Now listen. The King plans to kill the boy and sell you. The camel is much better. Here is your satchel of food and a water carrier. It is a fair price. Now go!' Johin felt the same strong hands jerking at the ties around her feet, and a knife nicked the skin on her ankle. She gasped, but the cloth in her mouth prevented her from calling out.

'Go!' the voice commanded, and a sliver of cold, grey light appeared, as a portion of the tent wall was pulled up.

Johin looked around frantically for Manny. She could see nothing in the gloom. She shoved their old glass bottle into the satchel and dived for the gap.

The withered face of the old grandmother peered in at her, beckoning desperately. Johin flattened herself into the sand and slithered through the opening. Pulling the blanket out after her, Johin ran as fast as she could to the nearest clump of rocks. Crouched in their shelter, she pulled the choking wad of cloth from her mouth. As she slumped onto the sand to catch her breath, she saw she was not alone.

A tall, skinny figure in old linen shorts was folding his blanket into a neat kilt around his waist.

'Good, you have the bottle and the satchel. Now hurry,' he whispered. 'Roll up your blanket, there's not a second to lose!' Manny turned towards the Wanderer's encampment, held out his hands in a gesture of farewell, and sang a soft note in their direction. 'What are you doing now?' snapped Johin. 'I thought we were in a hurry!'

'Blessing them,' he said simply.

'Blessing them! When they wanted to kill you and to sell me as a slave? You must be crazy.'

'They also fed us, sold us a good blanket at a fair price, gave us shelter for the night and rescued us from death and worse. Does not that deserve a blessing?'

'But what about the King?' protested Johin. 'He was evil!'

'The River will meet him on his own terms,' said Manny quietly. 'Now we must run!'

Manny grabbed the satchel in one hand, and Johin's wrist with the other, and dragged her down a long hillside, over a stone wall and up another slope. They crawled low at the crest of the hill, then slithered down into a wide, dry river bed. She felt as if her lungs would burst, her legs burned, and she was so weak she could have wept. But Manny kept dragging and cajoling her to keep running.

Ahead there was nothing but baked, cracked mud, and huge, lonely rocks like massive broken teeth scattered across the wide valley bottom. They ran with agonising spurts from wild shaped boulders to hidden crevasses. At last she collapsed in a limp heap. 'Go on without me,' she gasped, 'I can't move!'

Manny swung her up on his bony shoulders like a sack of flour. The world seemed to spin and dive insanely, until suddenly she was falling, bumping down a scree slope, scraping her arms and legs and cracking her head on a rock. Together they rolled and slid until they came to rest at the bottom of a deep gully. They lay panting and fearful, listening, hardly daring to breathe.

'I think we'll be all right now!' he said between gasps.

Johin pushed the hair and blood out of her eyes and looked up at him. Suddenly she burst into floods of tears.

'I've lost Nuffle!' she sobbed.

Her head was throbbing, her arms and legs were stinging and she felt sick. Large drops of blood welled up and splattered rhythmically from her head onto the back of her hand, but it was all nothing. Nuffle was gone.

Manny looked at her sadly for a few minutes. 'Don't you think he might be happier running free?' he asked quietly.

'No! she snapped rudely. 'I love him, he was all I had left in the world. You've taken everything else from me, now I've lost him too!' and she started crying uncontrollably.

Manny sighed and climbed doggedly back up the scree slope. Lying flat on his stomach, he could see the Wanderers' search parties scouring the hills on the other side of the valley. There were caves and plenty of hiding places that way. They obviously had not expected the fugitives to dash across a wide expanse of open land. With any luck they would be looking for a Sand boy and a Mud girl together. A Sand boy on his own might not be noticed.

Carefully he crept forward. High up in the burning golden sky was a small hawk. Manny whistled, and the bird closed its wings and dropped like a stone until it landed gracefully on Manny's outstretched wrist. He stroked its brown and gold feathers, and sang gently to it. After a minute or two, the bird rose and flew off in the direction of the Wanderers' camp.

'And don't eat it!' called Manny. But the hawk was gone.

Within a few minutes it returned, holding a very sorry, tiny, white bundle hanging like wet washing from the mighty talons.

'Well done and thank you, my fine friend,' said Manny, and rewarded him with a strip of dried meat from the satchel. 'May the Lightwater give you true flight!' he called to the rapidly rising shape, which turned and became a mere glinting speck in the morning sky.

Nuffle lay in Manny's lap, almost dead from the terror of his flight. Manny picked him up and stroked his fur, singing a gentle waking song to the little creature, then very tenderly, he carried him back to Johin.

Watching all the time for pursuers, Manny climbed back up the hill to the top of the scree slope. Johin lay flat at the top. She had watched, but had not understood.

Now she did not know what to say. She muttered 'Thank you,' but it seemed very shallow. Nuffle curled up in his familiar pocket, still shaking, his garnet-red eyes wide in fear.

Again they made their way down the scree, more slowly and carefully this time.

'Why did you escape, Manny?' puffed Johin, as she clambered down the steep side of the gully. 'I thought you gave your word not to.'

Manny gave his mischievous grin. 'I only said I wouldn't dream of it . . . and I didn't.'

'I thought from the way you were talking last night that you expected the Lightwater to work some magic to make them just *let* us go.'

'Wasn't what happened good enough for you?' Manny turned painfully to look at Johin's thin, tired face. It was mapped with sticky streaks of blood. She hung her head.

'We need food and a wash,' he said quietly. 'Then we must hurry. I fear another earthquake tonight.

The little rocky valley in which they found themselves was bare, yellow and desolate. They made a controlled slide further down the sides of the ravine. Manny seemed to be listening for something. He turned to his left and walked carefully for a short way.

'What . . .?'

Manny motioned to Johin to be silent. He closed his eyes and held up his arms, palms outwards, and turned in a small, silent circle. Then he stopped, opened his eyes and walked forwards a few paces. 'Give me a hand here, will you?' he said.

Together they tugged at a smooth egg-shaped boulder. It was only the size of a man's head, but it was wedged firmly between larger rocks. Beneath it was a damp patch. They scraped at the wet gravel until a small but clear pool filled the shallow bowl they had made.

Johin sat back on her haunches. She looked at Manny in amazement. 'How did you *know?*' she demanded. 'What was all that circle-turning stuff? Was it more magic?'

Manny was too busy drinking and washing to answer for a few minutes. 'It's a little sour-tasting, but it'll do,' he pronounced. 'Take a good drink, as much as you can hold, and wash that blood off, then I can have a look at the cuts and see if you're all right.'

Johin was too bewildered to speak. She took the still-terrified Nuffle out of her pocket, and put him down near the pool. He soon drank his fill, and started to wash himself.

At last when they were both clean and well watered, and Nuffle had calmed down, Manny pushed the stone over the pool again. 'It won't dry up completely that way, and it'll still be there for someone else.'

He paused and looked around. 'No, it's not magic. It is

an ancient skill of the Sand people to find water. That is one reason your people distrust us. Mud people are terrified of anything done by the senses or simply by listening to the River. They believe that if something can't be measured, it must be evil or unreliable. It's only jealousy, really. It's just a matter of silence and skill.'

Manny put her head on one side and looked hard at Johin. She felt almost as if he was trying to *think* his knowledge into her head. 'All you need is the patience to learn it. First you close your eyes: what a place looks like can be deceptive. Then you listen carefully for any tell-tale sounds of water, then you "feel" for the moisture which may be there. That's why I hold my hands out; the palms of the hands are very sensitive.'

'How can you *feel* it?' asked Johin, quite lost. 'Everything's so very dry.'

'Exactly!' said Manny. 'What is driest? Dry or very dry?'

Johin hesitated. It seemed a very strange question. 'Very dry, I suppose.'

'So all you have to do is to search for where the air doesn't feel *quite* so dry. You see, it's very simple really.'

Johin shook her wet hair in the sun. 'Why did you go to the trouble of finding this pool when you have your never-emptying bottle? The Wanderers gave us a water carrier, too. Anyway, your water is better than this, and it's much less effort finding it.'

Manny shook his head. 'It's because this water *is* here, that we didn't need the Pool of Making's water. That is only for real emergencies. The River always gives us what we *really* need, so it's best not to be greedy with its gifts. If you think about it, if we'd used the Wanderers' water carrier, there wouldn't have been enough water to wash. We would have had to find water to refill it before we could set off, anyway.'

He put his hand to Johin's throbbing head. 'Let me see that cut,' he said gently. He eased her hair into a parting, and followed the course of an ugly gash behind her right ear.

He whistled a little. 'That must hurt,' he said. 'Now, don't move.'

Without saying a word, he gently traced the line of the cut with his finger, then, with a little water from the Pool of Making, he closed the wound. The throbbing lessened, and the bleeding stopped.

Johin looked at him wide-eyed. After a minute she said, 'Why do you do things for me when I'm so rotten to you?'

'Because you're not worth it, perhaps?' He grinned a little. 'You know all about helping people who aren't worth it, don't you? Anyway,' he stood up and stretched, 'we have a long way to go; we haven't come nearly as far as I'd hoped. We can eat breakfast as we go.'

Johin reluctantly got to her feet and made sure Nuffle was safely in her pocket, and they set off northwards.

10
Dream Song

It was the sound of chanting that made Manny hurry.

They had walked all day, often in silence, to save energy and water. They were still going north, but journeying well to the west of the River's course, taking unmarked hill paths to avoid being seen.

They rested in the early afternoon. Even the strongest and most well-fed traveller could not have stood that heat. They found shade from a copse of drought trees, settled deep in a valley of dry yellow grass and blue-black shadows. They ate the Wanderers' black bread and gritty goat's cheeses which had been made in intriguing little moulds to look like birds and fat little animals. There was also fruit and long strips of black, rubbery, dried meat. Johin looked a little worried.

'It is good, you'll like it,' Manny promised her. Nuffle did not seem impressed by the dried meat either, and contentedly nibbled bread crumbs.

After eating, they slept in the shade.

Johin's dreams were woven through with a strange, monotonous moaning sound.

Suddenly, the sound became clear. It was voices singing the ancient chants of wisdom. A band of Sand people was making its way slowly and solemnly down the hillside.

Manny was already on his feet, giving Johin a friendly jab in the ribs with his toe. He was beaming with pleasure.

'Come on, we shall have good company for the afternoon!'

Johin was not pleased. What was wrong with *her* company for the afternoon? She called Nuffle, who had been investigating an ants' nest, picked up her blanket, and walked sullenly and slowly after Manny.

As she had feared, she did not like the small group of Sand people. There were three families, with half a dozen children between them. Their song was dull, and the children solemnly kept time with simple instruments of sticks and tiny brass cymbals which clattered rather than rang. They stank and, what was worse, they had no manners.

Of course, they were all over Manny. Although he was no close relation, they always treated one of their own race as a long-lost brother or sister.

Johin was introduced, but she could not stand the way they kept trying to peer into her eyes. She felt as if they were trying to dig inside her. Johin offered her hand limply, because she felt she ought to, but only one of the senior women took it.

Silently Johin walked at the back of the group, listening hard to what Manny was saying, and wishing so much he would talk to *her*. He was *her* friend. *She* had rescued him.

The more hurt she let herself become, the more angry she grew. She did not like the shy children who came to offer her dried fruit. She thought they were laughing at her, and she shouted at them. Her throat began to swell and tighten, her eyes began to sting, and by the time they had set up camp on a good site with plenty of drought trees and a small pool of water, she felt ill and headachy. The blanket weighed heavily. Her back ached, and once again she wished she had never left her home.

The whole afternoon, Manny had been light-hearted and full of songs and stories. By evening she almost hated the sound of his voice. She wished he would go away if he wasn't going to be with her. He had *said* she wasn't worth being nice to: why had he not left her in peace at home, and gone on his silly, useless quest with his precious Sand people instead?

Johin fell in a heap rather further from the campfire than she would have liked to have been. One of the children brought her a bowl of water and a handful of dried fruit. She ate it greedily, although she was well aware that they had probably given her more than they could really afford, and she hankered for more.

All evening her hunger, thirst and anger grew inside her until they seemed to be shouting deafeningly. In fury she buried her head under her blanket and went to sleep.

From the depths of her dreams, Johin heard someone calling her. She felt compelled to waken. It was still fairly early in the evening, the stars were very bright and the night was cold. The Sand people were huddled around the fire, listening to a cool, clear voice.

It was not singing words, but pictures and images so vivid, that once again Johin found herself within the song. She wanted to cry all over again, from the sheer beauty of the voice, and the hugeness and joy of the stories it sang.

Then she sat up with a start. The voice was Manny's. He was singing the Song of the Lightwater: wordless, but penetrating every fibre of her being. He sang, and she felt as if he were singing to her alone.

In the dream-song, Johin found herself in a new, waking world. She was sitting on a small grassy island in the middle of a wide rushing river. The water was ice-cold and gloriously clear, laughing, commanding and singing as it went. Out of it, all along its banks, crawled creatures and beings of every imaginable kind, and where it watered, rich vegetation was discovering itself. Bright green and deep blue plants uncoiled, spreading themselves wide and full in the new-born heat of the sun.

The island on which she sat seemed to be floating and rushing with the river, like a small, living boat. A swift eddy drew her aside to where slack water was creating a small still pool. At first all she could see was a cool, bright light.

Strangely, it did not hurt her eyes, and as she gazed into it, she saw Manny peering down into the water. It wasn't Manny the ordinary scrawny Sand boy: he looked very different; but it was definitely Manny. Smiling at his own likeness, he leant over the water, and his reflection sank into the deep, rich red mud at the bottom. Soft as a wave, the mud began to stir, to take shape and to move. The figure opened her eyes and looked up into the light. A breeze stirred the leaves of the overhanging trees, and the girl made of mud breathed, and sat up.

Johin was filled with delight for it was herself, herself as she ought to be, in the same way that she could now see Manny as he really was.

Then the joy faded, for she saw herself stretch out her hands and strike out poisonously at the River and all its beauty. Her face twisted in anger and greed. Manny called to her, but she turned and laughed spitefully at him. She sprang to her feet, and with one bound she leapt on to the bank. She was free of the River, and there, waiting for her was someone else . . . a tall, shining figure she had seen somewhere before. He was pulling—summoning—binding her. She could not get free of him.

All around her the water dwindled, there was death everywhere, and the land turned to dust. The planet became a sad, shrunken mockery of the place it had been. The song seemed to take a hundred years to sing, but at last the voice dwindled in sorrow, until Johin found herself sitting up, awake, cold and lonely, under the stars.

The family of Sand people left early, as they preferred to travel in the cool half-light. They were making their way to an ancient town two days' journey away. They had heard rumours of water there, and even some workable land. It was worth investigating. Manny found it hard to wake Johin. In the end he had to tug her heavy blanket and tip her onto the sand. Even then she moved only because she found herself nose-to-nose with a large black spider. She got up very quickly. Her dreams and visions shattered in a moment.

'I thought you were meant to be kind and loving, Manny, you horrid boy! I was asleep, you pig!'

Manny shrugged and grinned. He pointed at the thin line of small purple ants making their way across Johin's blanket. 'You can stay there if you like,' he said, 'but I wouldn't!'

'*Do* something!' she shrieked. 'I *hate* purple ants. Their bite makes me itch for days!'

'Why do you expect *me* to do anything about it?' asked Manny, still grinning broadly.

'Because you're a know-all, that's why. And because you're laughing at me and because ... because ... I'm scared, Manny. Please!'

'Try moving,' he said, lifting his eyebrows in an infuriating way.

Johin grabbed the blanket and started flapping it uselessly. Manny took the other end firmly and said, 'Calm down, Johin. Let me *help* you.'

Johin subsided. Manny helped her to pull the blanket taut, and showed her how to beat it like a drum until all the ants were free. Together, they rolled the blanket up, and strapped it into a tight bundle. Nuffle perched on Johin's shoulder and Manny shared out rations as they walked.

She knew that eventually she would have to forgive

him for being right. At last she broke the silence. 'Where are we going today?' she asked breathlessly as she tried to keep pace with his long strides. 'And do we have to walk so fast?'

Manny smiled and slowed down. 'I thought we'd go the same way as the Sand people went. I want to see this magnificent town of Greenhevel too. It is odd that there is water there, but no one seems to stay. I have heard strange tales of ghosts and weird creatures that guard it, but who knows what tales people make up to scare others away from water? people don't like sharing much.'

Johin was silent. Inside, she was wincing. She thought she had seen the last of those awful Sand people. And now Manny was running off as fast as he could to meet up with them again. More of their rudeness, more of Manny not paying her any attention.

'What's the matter?' Manny coaxed.

'Nothing,' she shrugged, avoiding his gaze.

'Why were you so jealous of me last night? Why didn't you join in with us? You were very rude and unkind, you know.'

'Me rude! That's rich!' she flared. 'They wouldn't even shake hands, let along talk to me! They kept peering into my eyes! I didn't like it! They gave me the creeps, if you must know!'

Manny shook his head. 'Shaking hands is a custom of *your* people. We open our hands like this, to show we have no weapons, then we look each other in the eye to show we are open-hearted. It is just another way of doing things. The fact they did not make a fuss of you was a compliment. It showed they felt you were their equal, they treated you as one of them. They accepted you as my sister, and expected you to join in. If they had bowed and touched their foreheads to you, and called you "madam", it would have been the greater pity. That would have meant that they did not accept you.

'As it was, you wasted a whole evening hurting yourself inside, as well as grieving my friends, just because you were jealous of me taking notice of someone other than yourself. Why did you do it? You know you can't own the Lightwater. You never used to be like this!'

Johin swallowed and said nothing. The truth was that at home she had been a bit of a celebrity. She had liked being important—the friend of Manny the water-maker. Here, she was no one special. If she could have run home at that moment, she would have, but there was nowhere to run to. She shook her head and bit her lip. A large tear rolled down her cheek. Instead of letting Manny cheer her up, she dropped behind. Manny hung back and waited for her. Then she rushed ahead, but she could feel him behind her.

She stopped and turned on him, red-faced and furious.

'Oh, go away, Manny, leave me in peace, you've ruined everything!' she stamped. Then clutching her bundle, and Nuffle, she ran as fast as she could along the track, sobbing her heart out.

She continued like that until the sun hung high and hot in the sky. When she decided to rest in the shade of rocks, Manny stayed well away from her, finding his own rock to shelter under. She was glad he had, because she knew that if once she looked into his green-blue eyes that were so like the deep, clear River-water of the dream-song, she would fall to pieces. She would have nothing to say. She knew that what he said was true, but she didn't want to let go of her fury and self-pity. It comforted her, even thought it hurt.

She determined that when they met the next camel train, she would ask the Wanderers to take her with them, even if it meant going to the slave market. Anything must be better than travelling day after burning day with this . . . this . . . Sand boy!

She took a pot-shot with a pebble at a lazy black scorpion that happened to be passing. Then she fell asleep.

Even in her sleep, Johin could not evade those eyes, the eyes of water—oh, she was so thirsty! She wanted a drink, but she just couldn't reach the clean, clear pools of water, she couldn't let herself anywhere near! It was so dangerous, but oh, how she needed to be there.

When she woke, the small leather water carrier the Wanderers had given them was by her feet, and Manny was gone.

11
Johin Alone

Johin called until she was hoarse.

The purple hills with their brown sand slopes just shook in the heat, and the flies pestered around her head.

Exhausted, she sat down hard on the baked earth. All she wanted to do was to cry herself home. She took one careful drink from the water carrier and wiped her eyes and nose on the skirt of her tunic.

'Now, I've got to think. Home is three, possibly four days back, and where Manny is heading is two days ahead. Home is certain, but is dangerous—even my parents wanted me to get away for a while. I can't go back, not yet, anyway.

'Manny is an annoying, big-headed pig, and I don't want to go with him, but if I can find this deserted town he was talking about, he needn't know I'm there. I can just find somewhere to squat, and look after myself there for a while until it's safe to go home. Manny can go on his lunatic goose chase with the Sand people. What have I got to do with them anyway?'

Johin rolled up her blanket neatly and tightly. Nuffle ran behind a nearby rock, and refused to be caught. After a long, hot chase the rebellious mouse was returned to her pocket. This made her even crosser as she turned north.

The track was covered with a light scattering of soft sand, and the marks of Manny's large, rather flat feet were easily traceable.

'If I don't rest in the afternoon, I might even make the journey in less than two days!' she thought. But within half an hour she was already tired. At the end of an hour she was again wishing she had never left home. But she trod steadily on in the raging heat.

She rested a short time in a scanty copse of drought trees, and ate as much fruit as she could find. They were small and tough, with exceptionally hard, dry skins. The dull grey-green leaves rattled and clattered overhead in a stiff breeze. It felt like the beginning of a sandstorm. The faint distant rumbling of an impending earthquake frightened her. Her water was getting dangerously low, and there was no real shelter within sight.

She knew her only chance was to find some kind of wind-break—rocks, a cave, anything. The hill country she had left that morning had now opened out into a wide, flat plain, and the wind was getting stronger by the minute. She could think of nowhere she had passed that day which would afford her real shelter. Her only hope was to go on.

The sand began to rise and to blow hard. Soon her bare legs were smarting with the roughness of the sand flinging itself relentlessly at her skin. Her eyes were stinging, she could not breathe, and still the wind blew harder.

Suddenly, to her horror, Johin realized she could no longer see the way. She was wandering aimlessly into a nightmare of spinning dust and sand. In desperation, she sank to her knees and pulled the blanket over her whole body. Manny had been right, it did keep the sand out. At least she could breathe, although it was stiflingly hot and stuffy.

She didn't dare lift a corner for more air. The slightest gap under the blanket sent jets of burning sand bursting into her tiny sanctuary. As she lay on the ground, she could feel the erratic shaking and grinding of the earth in its depths.

She knew Manny would be in pain; he always was when there was an earthquake. It was something to do with him being part of the River, and the River dying. She did not understand it, but for a few brief seconds she almost wished she could be with him to fetch him a drink, for his pain would be terrible. Then she remembered what an unreasonable pig he had been, and went back to thinking about herself.

She was really frightened ... even more frightened than when Brilliance had appeared in the cave. She hadn't been alone then, Manny had been with her, so it had been all right. Now she was alone.

Where was he? Why had he gone off in such a huff? It was cruel of him to leave her alone and unprotected in this dreadful place. How had she been so taken in by him? Why did everyone trust him so much? All he did was to stir everyone up then disappear. It was wrong, *wrong*, WRONG!

Then the heat and lack of air overcame her, and Johin fainted.

When she woke, the blanket had been pulled back, the storm and the earth tremors had passed, and a small group of Sand people was standing over her looking worried.

'Are you all right, Madam?' said one.

'We've brought you water and food!' said another.

Johin took a good drink and ate the food.

Something inside told her they were offering the last of poor supplies. She didn't care. She was one of the Mud people and deference was due to her. Sand people were built for that sort of meagre existence; they had come from the desert sands. She, on the other hand, needed to be kept moist and sleek. That was the way the Light had made her.

She got up and brushed herself down, rolled the blanket and thanked the Sand people politely. She ignored their greetings of outstretched hands and strode off across the sands.

'Madam,' called an Elder, a small greyish lady, 'where are you going?'

Johin hesitated. How much should she tell? She didn't want these Sand people to share the luxury of living near water.

She turned and smiled slyly. 'I'm going to Greenhevel, a deserted town a day or so from here. I'm going to meet a friend there . . . but don't follow me. I've heard dreadful stories about the place. Some say it's haunted!'

'Well, if you're going to Greenhevel, you're going the wrong way,' said the Elder deferentially. 'We're going there too. The point you have to aim for is the left of that brown hill on the horizon. Do you see? Why don't you join us? You'd be welcome, and much safer!'

Johin hesitated, but she knew that their powers of finding water were her only hope. She could always find a way of making them move on later. 'Thank you. I will,' she said.

When it came to their evening meal, everything was shared equally. Johin grudgingly offered her water carrier. There was one drought fruit and about half a dozen grains of wild wheat each. Nuffle would have to go hungry.

The only child with the group was a tiny little girl of about seven summers called Misha. Her arms and legs were as thin as sticks, but she was sweet-natured and friendly. When they all sat down to eat, the child caught sight of Nuffle, and without thinking, clambered carelessly between the adults to stroke him. As she landed awkwardly on the ground, she caught Johin's hand with her thin little legs, and all the wheat grains tumbled into the sand.

Johin felt herself go cold with fury. Everyone went silent, and looked in terror at her to see what she would do. As Johin raised her hand to hit the child hard across the head, the evening light caught the thin hard bones of Misha's face and the deep, dark eyes looking up with a timid smile. 'Please Madam, will you share my drought fruit?' she asked.

Johin nodded and lowered her hand. 'It wasn't really your fault,' she muttered. She took the fruit, but could hardly swallow it. The flesh was bitter and rotten and stuck in her throat. But she made herself eat it. 'I've got to keep my strength up,' she told herself firmly. 'We'll get some more for the child tomorrow.'

A shelter was made with half a dozen or so light, flexible poles tied together at the top. As Manny had done, the Sand people took off their kilts and unfolded them to spread over the poles, making a tepee.

As night came on, the little group split up. The Elder slept with Misha's mother under one blanket, and the two brothers under the other.

159

After the heat, they were cold in their threadbare linen shorts and tunics. Johin gently pulled Misha under her own new thick rug, and tried to sleep. However she lay, she felt a hard lump under her hip. 'I must have caught a stone in my pocket,' she thought, irritated. But it was no stone, it was one of the small hard cheeses from the Wanderers' satchel. What luck! With everyone else asleep she could have it all to herself. It was so tiny, it would be difficult to share anyway. Nuffle could have the crumbs.

Barely had her teeth sunk into the delicious morsel, than a tiny movement and a whimper next to her made her freeze. 'What's the matter, Misha? Are you cold? Do you want to cuddle up to me?' she asked.

'No,' came a barely audible whisper. 'I'm so hungry, lady.'

Johin bit further into the cheese and broke off the rest. Taking the little girl's thin fingers she wrapped them around the remaining piece. 'Here, suck that, it'll do you good.'

With that, Johin turned over and tried to sleep, but the sucking sounds made her feel even more hungry. 'What's the point of saving the child?' she thought. 'We've no chance of reaching Greenhevel with no rations and her in that state. If she dies tonight, the rest of us might make it.'

She slipped in and out of dreams and waking. Every time she closed her eyes, she kept seeing Manny: Manny lying almost dead on the ground, Manny when she carried him, Manny when he woke and gave her water, Manny holding her deep in the River, Manny saving Nuffle and healing her cut, Manny as he *really* was.

Suddenly she could bear it no longer. She sat bolt upright, '*Manny!*' she shouted into the night air, '*Manny!*'

The tiny child next to her was making that horrid rasping sound that Manny had made when he was dying. Frantically she tore another strip from her tunic, and using the Wanderers' water, she tried to revive Misha by squeezing drips into her mouth. It had worked on Manny and the Sand babies at home.

This time there was no response. The child's breathing got worse, and she was terribly hot. Misha was dying. She needed water from the Pool of Making.

It was all Manny's fault. If he had been here, he could have given her water from the Pool. He'd have done something, sung something . . . If only he hadn't gone off in a sulk!

Johin crawled out of the tent, and struggled out into the night. There was a streak of dawn on the horizon, she thought she could just see the edge of the hill near

Greenhevel. She would go to get Manny and *make* him face his responsibilities. He must *do* something! He must restore the Pools of Making everywhere. All this talk of going to the source was just an excuse not to do what was most needed. She would *make* him come back and help Misha and her family. *Now.*

She hesitated before leaving her precious blanket. It would slow her down to have to carry it, and Misha needed it. Faithful Nuffle was still sleeping soundly in her pocket. Johin took a last desperate swig at the water carrier. There were a few drops left in it. She would take it in case she found water.

Just then a weak voice came from inside the tepee. 'Where are you going, Madam?'

'I'm going to get Manny, I'm going to get help.'

'Manny? Oh yes,' and there was silence.

Johin set off towards the outline of the hill which was becoming stronger as the day dawned. It didn't look far, she thought. She might just make it. She put her head down and strode off at a steady rate towards the left of the hill, trying to think of anything but how thirsty she was, and how ill and tired she felt.

At first she tried to think of Misha, and her dark, hopeless eyes. Then she tried to think of home and the greenness by the Pool of Making. But she kept coming back to thinking about herself and what a beast she had been.

Manny was right, she *had* been jealous. She had been rude and mean to the Sand people. *She* had sent Manny away; *he* hadn't left *her.* He had given her food and drink when she didn't deserve it. He hadn't left her helpless; somehow he had made sure somone had found her in the sandstorm. It was all her fault! She could have been safe with him in Greenhevel by now ...

Greenhevel! Where was it? She had been so wrapped in

her thoughts she had forgotten to take her bearings. Now the hills were wrapped in more sand and dust, and another storm was sweeping across the plain.

'*Manny!*' she shouted. 'Manny! Help me!'

12
Risking the Magic

Johin had no blanket to protect her and no water. The clouds were sweeping in quickly. The sand was rising to thrash and cut at her already sore arms and legs.

'Manny! Where are you? How do I know if I'm even going in the right direction? I haven't even got a blanket, I'm done for if I don't find you! Manny!' she pleaded into the wind.

'When you were here everything was all right. I know it's *me* that's been the pig ... I'm sorry! Where are you? I need you ...' Her mouth filled with sand as she called hopelessly into the lashing wind. She did not dare call out again. Spitting sand, and terribly thirsty, she trudged on into the whirling cloud of white and yellow dust.

She found herself muttering inside the front of her tunic, 'I know you said I always have to think of you as being "in the middle of everything", Manny, but where's the middle?'

Instinctively she held out her arms in front of her, as if she were blind. 'I wonder if I can find you, like you found water? What is driest? Dry or very dry? Where is Manny? Where feels more Mannyish? I'll close my eyes. He said what a place looks like can be deceptive ... Then if I think of Manny, think of him being here, in the middle ... which way are you, Manny? This way! Oh, he's this way!!'

And to her surprise and joy she found herself walking firmly in one direction. He was this way, she just knew it!

She was glad to have to keep her eyes shut, for the sand would have blinded her within seconds. She staggered on and on into the yellow swirling nightmare. At last she sank to the ground, unable to walk or even breathe.

Suddenly, she was caught by a strong pair of arms and she found herself being pulled firmly along, until the wind died, the sand stopped and everything went quiet. She was safe, and being hugged by Manny.

They were in a small, cool cave. Outside, the storm roared on. Sheltered at last, Johin collapsed weeping, then slept, like a tiny child. Manny stroked her hair and softly sang the song that had called her.

After a little while he shook her gently. 'Johin, Johin, we can't rest here long, things are much too dangerous. Have some food and water, then we must hurry.'

Johin carefully wiped the sand from her eyes. She could hardly speak because of the sand clogging her mouth. Slowly, she said, 'I'd be glad of food, and I'm so desperately thirsty I could drink the whole River, but if it's water from the Pool of Making, I dare not drink. I would rather just die here.'

Manny rummaged in his satchel and gave her a soft, fresh drought fruit, half a black loaf and a small cheese. When he looked up he was smiling, kindly, but mischievously. 'Why won't you drink, my little cat?'

Johin shuddered. 'Cat isn't the half of it. I've been horrid to you, Manny. I *was* jealous, I chased you away, I thought all sorts of awful things about you ... yes, and about the River and the Light within the River. If it was just a cat you would turn me into, I wouldn't mind so much. But I'm scared I'm a really horrid sort of a "thing" inside. I'm scared of drinking your water—I can't!'

She sat in a crumpled heap of despair. 'If ... If you go back across the plain, the way I came, I'm not sure where ... you'll find four Sand people with a little girl.

The child is dying. Give *them* your water; they need it more than me. They were good to me, so the Pool won't work its magic on them.'

Manny stretched out his hand and touched her forehead where he had made the Mark. His fingers burned her gently. 'Are you so frightened of me, Johin?' he asked softly.

She looked up from her heap on the floor. His face was deep and kind. 'No, I'm not frightened of you. I trust you. I think I'm frightened of what's inside *myself*,' she said glumly.

'If you don't drink, you will die of thirst,' said Manny making her sit up. 'That "thing" that was inside you is left behind in the wind. It fled when you came looking for me—when you thought of me as "being in the middle", remember? If you're not afraid of me, drink. We must hurry, or else I will lose two friends because of thirst today.'

Johin drank the cool, wet, life-giving water. Timorously she examined her hands and feet. There was no change.

Manny laughed at her and held out his hand. 'Come on, you silly!' he said. 'You'll understand one day.'

Johin let herself be pulled to her feet. 'I'll eat as we go along,' she said, 'I feel as if I could run round the world! Oh, Manny, you and your Pool water, you are wonderful!' She gave him a hug and launched herself out of the cave mouth straight into the raging storm.

She was flung back as if she had run into a brick wall. 'Manny, it's impossible out there. What are we going to do? Misha is dying!'

Manny stepped up to the cave mouth and looked out into the cruel, swirling wind and sand.

'Be quiet now, that's enough!' he said simply. Then he stepped out into a calm sunny day, as a few wisps of dusty sand settled in fine layers on the rocks.

Not a hundred paces away was a stooping blanket-wrapped figure. As the wind fell, he straightened. He started, hesitated, and ran in a weary, jerking way towards Manny and Johin. 'Madam, you are alive,' he said. 'I followed you to make sure you were all right.'

'Thank you,' she said, suddenly self-conscious of the title of 'Madam'. As Manny had said, it made her feel uncomfortable and an outsider. 'Please call me Johin. Thank you for taking the trouble to come after me. As you see, the Lightwater took care of me. How is Misha?'

The young man motioned behind him. 'My brother Yaap is carrying her. I think she is still alive. When we heard you knew where Manny was, we followed you. There are many stories about his magic among our people.'

Johin nodded towards Manny who had been standing behind her. 'Here he is,' she said. 'I didn't think you would have the strength to bring Misha here. We were just on our way to find you.'

'Take me to her,' said Manny. 'I will do some of the carrying. Johin, you rest in the cave, you are exhausted.'

She was about to argue, but then realized she was tired. She was especially tired of arguing with Manny. Gratefully she sat in the cool of the cave. She put Nuffle on her shoulder. She liked the tiny trembling feeling of his minute claws against her skin, and the soft twitch of his whiskers against her face.

She must have slept, for it seemed no time at all before Manny strode into the cave, grimfacedly carrying a limp little bundle. He was followed by Misha's mother and grandmother, and the brothers Yaap and Arie. Silently Manny sat on a flat rock. He laid the precious bundle across his knee, and started to sing.

Johin searched briefly for the old glass bottle with water from the Pool of Making. Using a small tin cup provided by Misha's mother, she offered the water to Manny. 'You do it,' he muttered between breaths of the song.

Terrified in case she spilled a drop, and feeling that it should be Manny, not her, giving the life-water, Johin parted Misha's lips and poured a few drops into her mouth. The child's breathing was slow, noisy and painful. Johin felt for her. Manny held his long, thin hands just hovering over Misha's head and heart. The rhythm of his song seemed to be willing a stronger heartbeat into the child.

Suddenly he stopped singing, looked up and shouted, 'Get out, all of you!'

Everyone sat there, looking stunned and stupid. Manny stood up, almost in fury, and threw Misha at her mother. 'Get out, I say!' and he started pushing and thrusting the terrified Sand people out into the open. Johin grabbed for Nuffle. Then with all his strength, Manny threw his entire weight at her, knocking her clean out of the cave mouth. As he did so, there was a terrifying cracking sound. Heaving, grinding stone and rock dust filled the air, and the cave collapsed as another earthquake tore at the ground under their very feet.

'Run!' yelled Manny. 'Run to Greenhevel!'

13
Greenhevel

The ground seemed to shake itself, like a dog throwing off a blanket. Hot air blasted sand and dust in every direction, choking and blinding everyone.

Then the deafening noise stopped as suddenly as it had started. The dust settled, and the hillside where they had been was transformed. The cave had been a low triangular space, under a heavy overhanging ledge. This had been shaken loose and skewed to one side, making the cave mouth look like a leering grin.

'It looks like Brilliance,' gasped Johin. 'He's laughing at us! He's killed Manny . . . *NO!*' and with that she bounded forward to the pile of fallen rocks.

The two Sand men were already there, desperately pulling at slabs with their bare hands. Johin thrust Nuffle into her pocket, and turned to Misha's terrified mother. 'Go and get help!' she yelled. 'There should be more Sand people in Greenhevel!'

The woman looked bemused and hopeless. Transfixed, she stared wide-eyed at the scene. 'Get Misha away from here, quickly!' yelled Johin. 'Get help! *RUN! PLEASE!*' Johin flapped her arms at the poor woman. Suddenly she seemed to understand. Clutching the child as tightly as she could, she turned and ran towards Greenhevel.

Johin and the men pulled and tugged at the rocks until their fingers bled. All the while, Misha's grandmother sat with her grey blanket pulled over her shoulders, hugging her knees. Rocking backwards and forwards, she droned a monotonous chant into her lap.

Suddenly Johin's temper cracked. 'Oh stop that noise, you stupid old woman! I can't concentrate! Go to Greenhevel if you can't help here!'

The woman did not hear. She just kept on rocking and droning, as if there was nothing else to do in the whole world.

Yaap laid his hand quietly on Johin's arm. 'Don't stop her, Madam Johin, she is singing the Song of Holding. If she stops, the rocks may fall further. All our lives depend on her.'

Johin tossed her head indignantly. '*My* life is protected by the Lightwater. I don't need *your* spells. The River will rescue Manny!'

Yaap was almost crying. 'Madam Johin, please listen to the Song. Can't you *hear* that it is part of the Song of the Lightwater? *All* our songs come from the River. If we do not work with all the powers and strength the River has given us, then the River will not be *able* to rescue Manny. The Lightwater has put his life in our hands. Can't you see?'

Johin bit her lip as she felt tears welling in her own eyes. 'I am sorry,' she said quietly. 'I should have listened. I should have recognized the Song. I *have* heard it before.'

'Look!' called Arie. 'I think that's a hand!'

With every last sweating bit of strength they had, the three of them pulled away a small slab. Underneath was Manny's head and shoulders, white and yellow with dust. He was caught under a flat stone which had protected him from being completely crushed. He was still alive, but they could do nothing more without stronger arms to lift the stone.

'He needs water from the Pool,' said Johin. 'Where's the bottle?' Then she realized with horror that she had dropped it when Manny had pushed her out of the cave. Searching frantically, she found dark green glass shards and a bottle neck . . . and blood.

Her heart missed a beat. She went cold and could not breathe. Manny had fallen on the bottle, and it had shattered underneath him. A slow trickle of water and blood oozed out from under his chest.

Yaap lifted Manny's shoulder slightly. Underneath it was the rest of the bottle, still intact. Johin gently eased it free. Wordlessly, Arie handed her the squashed tin cup she had used for Misha. With utmost care, Johin poured the last few drops of Pool water from the unbroken half of the bottle into the cup. But Manny was unconscious. Johin dampened her fingers and pushed them between his lips. Nothing happened.

Heavy with grief, she willed her hands to pour the last precious drops into the safety of the Wanderers' leather bottle which still hung from her shoulder.

Then everything went red, and Johin fainted.

When she awoke, Johin was lying on a grassy slope above a small lake. The grass was rough, coarse and scratchy, not like the soft growth around the Pool of Making, and it was a strange, still, dead sort of place. There were no birds, and scarely any insects. It was silent, apart from the singing of the Sand people, a shadow's length away.

Johin sat up and looked around. Misha's family had found the group of Sand people that Johin and Manny had walked with a few days before. They had made camp, and there was a fire, and a smell of food cooking.

The Sand people were kneeling or sitting in a large circle around a small hump on the grass. They were singing a low, steady song.

Johin listened. It was still the Song of the Lightwater.

She knew that now. Oddly she felt as if she had always heard it, inside her, all her life. But this part of it she had never heard. It was . . . a Song of Calling . . . Calling . . .

'Manny?' she said softly.

Misha's mother turned to her, and with a small smile, put her finger to her lips.

Johin crawled across and squeezed into the circle. In the centre, Manny was lying still, but breathing. He lay on a woven mat of straw, and his kilt had been unwound to cover him.

Johin listened again. She wanted to be able to understand for herself what was happening. If the Lightwater really flowed in her, she should be able to understand.

Soon she picked up the slow rising and falling of the tones. One or two higher voices curled a soft pleading throughout the chant. It sounded like a mother calling for a lost child on a hillside at night. If Manny had been anywhere above the ground, he would have heard it, and the heartrending call would have led him home.

Then one of the older men sang two or three very deep notes which hung in the air like the thrilling sounds of joy and time. Johin felt that if Manny had been in the depths he would have heard those notes, they engraved themselves so deeply on the hearer.

But Manny did not stir.

Very softly and gently, the Sand people lessened their song, until only one voice a bit wobbly and rather flat, was left singing. Suddenly and abruptly it stopped. Johin gasped. It was *her*. She had been singing. She had never in her life sung before, and there she was, singing one of the Sand people's sacred chants. She hadn't even realized she was doing it. All she knew was that she wanted Manny to live. He *had* to live. So much depended on him.

She blushed. 'I'm sorry . . .' she stammered.

But far from looking angry, the whole group was

smiling. 'Not at all,' said a stoop-backed Elder. 'You sing our songs very well. You have the feel for them. That is very important.' The Elder nodded her head slowly, and the group rose to their feet and went about their business.

Misha's grandmother came and put her arm around Johin. The old lady was a full head shorter than Johin. Her scalp was bald on top, but creamy white hair lay thick and curly around the base of her neck, where it was scraped together in a knot. She looked up intently into Johin's face with piercing green eyes. 'Come and talk with me.' The thin parchment-like hand pressed on Johin's shoulder and compelled her to sit. There was huge strength in that hand, despite its age and frailty.

'What's-the-matter-with-Manny-and-how's-little-Misha?' Johin's words all tumbled out at once.

The old woman handed Johin a leather flask of water, and some bread. 'All in good time. I will tell you everything,' she said. 'Eat, and listen.'

The old lady looked up towards the escarpment of the hills. Johin stared at her tortoise-like neck, and the tight, fair skin which clung to her face bones. She was so calm. Johin did not dare speak until she was spoken to.

When the old lady had finished her long reflection on the hills, she turned and looked at Johin. She breathed deeply. 'Put your mind at rest, Misha is recovering. We think she will live. If we can find enough food and water here, we can rest here awhile, and we may regain our strength.'

Johin interrupted, her mouth full of dry bread. 'But there is plenty of water, a whole lake! I have never seen so much, and there must be good growth here... Why should you worry about whether there's enough?'

The old lady smiled and the skin across her face tightened into rich folds around her eyes and mouth. She looked as if she spent her entire life listening. Johin decided that she was beautiful.

At length she waved her long bony hand towards the lake. 'This water is not good,' she said simply. 'Many years ago Greenhevel was famous for all the wonderful things that were made here. But the poisons came. Slowly, the waters thickened and went sour. The birds and animals left or died, the trees shrivelled from their roots upwards, and the town became silent.

'If we can find fresh springs that have not been spoiled, flowing from above the level of the lake, then all will be well. Some of the young people are out looking now.'

Then she fell silent again.

Johin stared hard at the green, still waters of the lake. It *was* thick and dull-looking. There was no light or sparkle. The old lady was right. The water was dead. It was indeed a ghostly place. The tales were not unfounded.

Suddenly Johin snapped her head round and grasped the old woman's arm tightly. 'Manny? What of Manny? Why were you all calling him? Where is he? I can see his body over there in those disgusting old shorts and terrible blanket . . . but where is *he*?'

The old lady showed no flicker of change in her gaze, still and calm as a hawk in mid-flight. 'Manny is not dead,' she said quietly. 'But we fear his spirit is still trapped under terrible rocks somewhere, as his body was.'

'He will be all right, won't he?' Johin willed her to say 'yes'. She grasped the thin yellowing arm too tightly and peered into the ancient face, forcing her to meet her gaze.

'I do not know. I cannot see,' she said simply.

Johin stood up. She wanted to argue, and *make* the old lady promise that Manny would be well, but Johin knew that it would achieve nothing. With the Sand people, answers came when they were prepared to give them.

She stretched and looked around. This would have been a beautiful place if it had not been so eerie. The sun was setting. Ochre and white grasses stretched whispering down to the shore. The sand was pink and pale yellow, making a pretty, mottled ribbon edging the luminous green satin water. To their right were the dark shapes of Greenhevel.

The town was built of pink concrete, mixed from the sand of the lake bed. Long, dreary, flat-roofed buildings in exact, neat rows stretched over the lower slopes of the hill on which the town was built. Tall black chimneys pointed accusing fingers into the sky. In the centre was a huge white globe, nestling on the town like the massive egg of a malevolent bird.

Johin gasped. 'What is *that*?'

The old lady did not even stir to look. 'That is how they made their power. It was very strong, and with it the people here could do anything they set their minds to achieve. But it was also the source of their poison.'

'Is it dead?' asked Johin nervously.

At last the woman looked round at it. 'No, it will not die in our lifetime, or the next. In many, many years to come it will die slowly. But perhaps it will have killed us first, so we will not be here to celebrate its death.' Then she was silent.

Johin thanked the old lady rather awkwardly, in Sand people fashion, with outspread hands, then she turned to go.

The old lady called after her, 'I think *you* might know how to call Manny. Do you, Madam Johin?'

14

The Moon on the Rocks

Johin had an uncomfortable lump in her throat. Why had the old Sand woman thought that she, a Mud girl, might know how to call Manny? Why her? It did not make sense.

Surely the Sand people were the ones who guarded the ancient wisdom and its secrets. If there were magic or Songs of Calling to be known, the Sand people would know them. She was new to the ways of the River. She was bothered and frightened. She wanted to be alone. Once she would have said she wanted to think. Now she knew she wanted to listen.

She turned away from the camp, and set off for the hills. From her position on the lower slopes of a rock escarpment just above the camp, she could see one of the Sand people sitting next to Manny, playing a reed pipe to him. Groups were settling around fires for the night. Here and there, little grey tepees had been put up for the elderly and the children. The night was still, and in the gathering dark she could see the clear glow of the green lake. It made her uneasy.

Determinedly, she climbed the rocks until she reached the road they had come by that morning. Twisting off to the left, and skirting the hill into the dark, it looked as if it went into the belly of the night itself.

Johin shivered, and wished she had thought to bring her blanket. Nuffle was nibbling at her leg through her pocket. She took him out and rubbed her tired face on his silky fur. He was comfortingly warm. 'We've got to go back to that cave, Nuffle,' she told him. 'We've got to find out how to call Manny, and I think that might be the place to start.'

Since the earthquake, the ground had become treacherous. Many times she slipped and cut herself on loose, sharp rocks. Thousands of years of sand and storm would one day soften the stony edges. But tonight they were freshly-sharpened knives against her legs.

Johin stuffed a protesting, squeaking Nuffle back into her pocket. She had to have both hands free to climb.

High above, the dust clouds started to part, and the moon shone through. The road ahead was fairly clear, cut deep into the hillside. She felt very small and alone. Fresh land slips scored huge, sharp, black and white craggy shapes, towering all around her, into the night. She felt as if she were being watched. Followed. Waited for.

Somehow, she kept going. Something told her she was going the right way. Suddenly, as the road took a twist, the cliffs levelled out to her right. To her left, sharply defined in the white full moon, was a dreadful face. Two or three times bigger than her leered the mocking, twisted grin of Brilliance, carved out of the living rock by the earthquake.

Johin froze and flattened herself behind a large jagged outcrop.

The face did not move or speak.

She crouched, scarcely breathing, for what seemed like hours, until at last she realized that it was not Brilliance. As the moon moved in its course, the patterns of light changed. There was no danger. It was simply the uncanny chance of the way the rocks had fallen. But it *was* the place where Manny had been crushed.

The sense of evil and foreboding did not lessen with

the changing moon. John walked out into the open and stood up straight. Brilliance might not be showing himself openly tonight, but she was certain that he wanted her to *think* he was there. He had left his portrait on the rocks but, like everything else he did, it was a sham, a distraction.

'Brilliance!' she shouted, 'Brilliance, are you here?' In the heavy silence, only a feeble echo challenged her back. She breathed very deeply, and called again.

'Brilliance, I have come to call Manny. I am going into that cave, because that is where I saw him last. That is where you tried to kill him. I know you are only a sham, a glitter—like the moon on the rocks. You cannnot touch the Lightwater.'

Her echoing words tumbled back at her, tossing themselves around the broken cliffs in a confused jumble of sharply broken sounds. She hesitated, wondering where she had found the courage to say all that—to challenge Brilliance openly, without Manny there.

Almost in response to her defiance, a small pile of stones slipped and cracked down behind her.

She jumped away terrified. Then she laughed softly. She should have known better than to shout out loud when rocks were unstable. Shouting could easily cause a fall.

With her heart in her mouth, she crept quietly into the remaining crack of the cave. It still had something of Brilliance's twisted leering grin from outside. She needed every scrap of courage to enter.

Softly she whispered into the still dark. 'The Sand people think your spirit is trapped somewhere, Manny. To be honest, I think you are just unconscious, and you'll be better soon. I don't know what the truth is, but I'm here to find out. I suppose you would just tell me to shut up and listen to the River within. I've tried that and I can't hear anything except my heart thumping. The water from the Pool of Making is lost. Oh Manny, I'm scared and tired. Where are you? *Do* I know how to call you?'

She sat down in the remnants of the cave, and hugged her knees until she slept.

When the first rays of light caught Johin's face and woke her, she was cold and stiff. Nuffle was licking at a few drops of condensation that had formed a damp puddle against the cave wall. She let him finish his drink, then she called him into her pocket.

'I wish I could drink like that,' she sighed. 'I have tried, but my tongue is too big. I just get a mouthful of grit, and then I'm thirstier than I was in the first place. Talking of which,' she said, getting up painfully, 'I must find water. I have a raging headache, and my stomach is tied in knots.'

Moving gently because of the black cuts and bruises which scored her arms and legs, she crawled out of the cave. The sun felt fresh and good. It was still early, for the oppressiveness of the day had not started yet.

She climbed along the road, with only one glance back at the cave. In the morning light, it had nothing of the fearful image which had terrified her before. She shook her head. Tiredness and weakness had played tricks on her.

Suddenly, she noticed a patch of fresh green, nestling in a dip in a hillside to her left. The road was easy to find, and the dead lake lay still and silent in the plain below. There was no danger of getting lost, so she left the road and struck out across the dry yellow and purple floor of the bare hillside.

The place must once have been very muddy, because deep cracks criss-crossed the hard-baked earth. It was like walking across a huge piece of crazed pottery. As she walked, the cracks became smaller, and fine shoots of green grass appeared.

Nuffle squeaked, and wriggled so much in her pocket she had to let him out. Delightedly, he flicked his long thin tail in the morning air, and scampered through what was rapidly becoming thick grass.

Johin stooped and felt the ground. It was soft. Even Nuffle's tiny claws left minute pin-prick marks in the ground. She quickened her pace, and ran the last few steps before throwing herself face down in a reed bed.

Black, sweet water oozed through the mud, and dark grey tadpoles darted away from her. This water was alive. It was fresh. It must be one of the springs the Sand people were looking for.

Laughing and crying all at once, she found a deeper part of the pool where the water was clear. She drank and ducked her head deeply. She washed her hair and face, then she took her sandals off and bathed her aching feet and legs.

The water was cool and good. At length she lay back in the sun and watched the light glistening on her legs as they dangled in the water. A few bees hummed gently in the rush flowers. She could not remember being so happy for a very long time, except maybe yesterday, when Manny had saved her from the sandstorm.

Suddenly she sat up, scaring away an inquisitive, luminous blue dragonfly. 'Manny! Oh, help, what do I do? I still haven't found what I came for!'

Urgently, she filled her leather water carrier and drank again from the pool. Poor Nuffle was stuffed back into her dusty pocket. Then, gathering a bundle of reeds from the pool edge, Johin scrambled back down the hillside.

There was no stream from the pool, although she could see that once there had been one. The water was drying in the heat before it could flow any distance. Following the shallow gully, she soon came to the lakeside.

With a shock she realized just how bad the lake water

was. The dull, flat greenness smelled putrid. Turning to her right, and following the edge of the lake, she spotted the Sand people's camp pitched on a flat shelf a little above the water.

She burst into a run, waving the bunch of green reeds in the air like a flag of spring. She dumped the heavy carrier on the ground. 'Water, I've found good water!' she shouted.

The younger, fitter Sand people ran towards her, hugging her with glee. Like a bountiful queen, she passed the water around freely. They laughed in sheer joy. The water was so good, it *made* one feel glad just to drink it.

Armed with bottles and skins and jars, every able-bodied person from the camp started the trek up the hillside, following the dry stream bed. Johin poured water for those who were too weak to walk, then she went over to Manny. She gave a drink to the singer who was watching him. 'I'll take over for a bit now, if you like,' she said, sitting next to Manny's pale, dry face.

She lifted his head. 'I seem to have done all this before,' she muttered to herself. Tearing yet another strip from her dirty and mutilated tunic, she started to give Manny water, drop by drop, pushing the wet rag between his lips and squeezing it.

Nuffle wriggled out of her pocket and ran across Manny's chest. In two bounds, he was up the boy's neck and on to his forehead. Carefully, the mouse began to wash Manny's dust-clogged eyes with his quick, darting little tongue.

After a while Johin stopped, and took another drink herself. She stared across at the dead, green water.

She did not know what else she could try. Why should the River have put Manny's life into their hands—into *her* hands? It all seemed so silly. If Manny died, everything would have been pointless, and the Planet would slowly crumble in dusty earthquakes.

Why didn't the River choose someone intelligent and wise to help Manny? Why had this happened anyway? Surely the River had *really* got it all wrong this time!

Even with the help of the Sand people, could she manage the long trek back to fetch water from the Pool of Making at Ardigham? Would Manny live long enough for her to make the journey? The earthquakes were getting worse!

Then in frustration, she lifted Manny's head, and shook his shoulder a little. 'Come *on*, Manny! You have work to do, remember? The Planet is in danger, *you* are in danger. Everything will end in disaster unless you wake up!'

There was silence.

She felt angry with her failure. She had tried. She had listened. She had faced Brilliance, or at least his shadow, alone. What *more* could she do?

'I know it's not water from the Pool of Making, Manny. I don't know where you are, whether part of you is somewhere else—or if you are just very ill, but you have got to keep your strength up. If you don't drink, you will die and Brilliance will have won!'

Johin buried her head in her knees and beat her fists on the ground. She felt so useless!

Suddenly, a dry, rasping voice next to her whispered, 'Oh, Johin, don't you recognize a Pool of Making when you see one?'

Manny had opened one eye, and was trying very hard to laugh.

Johin stared at him, then she looked at the leather bottle she was holding and shook it. It was at least three-quarters full, yet about thirty people had drunk from it.

Misha's grandmother, who had been sitting watching, came and touched Johin quietly on the shoulder. 'Let him sleep now. All will be well.' She drew Johin aside into a

117

stuffy little tepee. In it was her blanket and the Wanderers' satchel. Without needing to be told, Johin lay down and slept.

15
The Shadow of Brilliance

Johin was woken with a bowl of herb soup and wild honey bread. It tasted rich and golden and good. The old lady sat, silent as usual, in the doorway of the tepee. The tiny scrape of white hair at the back of her nodding head caught the glinting light of the sun.

When she had eaten, Johin tried to get up. 'Ouch!' she gasped. Every bone in her body ached and the scabs covering the cuts on her legs tugged and stung.

'Lie still,' said the old lady. Then she pulled back part of the tepee blanket so Johin could see out. She pointed up the bare hillside towards the new Pool. 'We have moved almost everything. You carried us yesterday. Today, we carry you.'

She stretched out her bony arm and beckoned to Yaap and Arie. With a few deft movements they had dismantled the shelter, and twisted the blanket over the poles to make a stretcher.

Johin was given no choice but to be carefully laid on it, and carried, swaying on sagging, bendy poles, up the hillside. Peering over the top of the stretcher she could see another group with a similar load, walking just a little ahead of them. She guessed it was Manny. She lay back, resigned to her captivity, although feeling a little queasy at the motion.

At last she heard the buzz and hum of voices, mingled with the laughing sound of children splashing. The stretcher was lowered. They had arrived. She lay still, listening to the wonderful noises of life.

The Sand people had already erected a little village of grey tepees. Here and there were hurdles made of woven reeds. Children were gleefully throwing clay daub at the hurdles to make them into solid walls. 'We will have homes here soon,' explained the old lady. 'Misha and her friends will have food and water. We may rest here.'

'What happens if others come and want to rest here?' asked Johin.

'Then they are welcome.'

Johin was worried. 'What if the Mud people want to come here too?'

The old lady sighed. 'Then they may share what the Lightwater has given to be shared.'

'But what if they bring guns and Water Guards and take it from you?'

The old lady stretched out her neck in her 'tortoise pose' as Johin called it, and scanned the hills in silence. Then quietly she said, 'It has happened before. It may happen again.' And she got up and went about her tasks.

Johin and Manny stayed in the growing village for several days.

Manny slipped in and out of consciousness, and fever gripped him for whole nights at a time, but slowly he was recovering.

One morning, Johin crawled out of her tepee, to see him standing by the Pool with a determined look on his face. Someone had washed and mended his shorts and his blanket. He looked cleaner and a little fatter, and even the hair on his half-bald head looked thicker and longer. An ugly red gash burned across his chest where the bottle had cut him. Despite healing herbs and water from this Pool of Making, the wound was still infected.

'Come on, Johin, we must be on our way. Time is running short, I can feel another earthquake coming. The River is almost dry. I must get to the source soon. We've lost time.'

Johin hesitated and looked back at the little village. 'It's funny, I feel so at home here now.'

'Don't you want to come?'

'I can't honestly say I *want* to come. It would be much easier to stay here ... but I know I've *got* to come, if you know what I mean.'

'No one will make you come,' Manny said. 'But I would be glad of your company. I think we may need each other yet.'

Johin nodded. 'I know. I have that feeling too.'

They collected their blankets, and filled a water bottle each. The Wanderers' satchel was stocked with black bread and a little clay jar of honey, sealed with wax.

Manny and Johin promised faithfully to come and rest if they returned that way. They walked down the hill and round a bend in the little valley. The road lay a short scramble below, but the village was still in sight.

Manny stopped and turned, and holding his hands out towards the village and its people, he sang one of his strange, wonderfully spine-tingling songs. This time, Johin knew what he was doing. On a flicker of wind from the camp she could hear the end of a Song of Parting, drifting down towards them.

Manny had always avoided the main road before. He had wanted to move without being seen. Now, he said, time was short. Speed was more important than cover.

The road swung to the right following the old shore-line, high above the stagnant puddle of the lake as it now was. Once the way had been wide and surfaced with water-smoothed cobbles, but years of crumbling drought and neglect had reduced the road to a track. Now travellers picked out a path amongst the rubble.

Every hour or two they passed huge stone troughs by the side of the road. For a price, donkeys and camels could drink there. Next to the troughs, in the shade of faded parasols, drink sellers sold water and tired-looking melon slices. Large black flies settled everywhere.

Occasionally, carts of grain and vegetables with attendant Water Guards passed them, trundling towards Dreeberg and Ardigham.

Sometimes they would exchange a word or two with fellow travellers. At other times, Manny would make Johin hide, breathlessly and without stirring, while Water Guard patrols went by on their hoverbikes.

Manny rested often, and drank as much as he dared. Some of the melon sellers would trade their wares for one of Manny's songs. Others spat in their faces. Somehow, he dragged himself through the day. By evening, they were about halfway around the lake, and heading for a deep gap in the distant mountain range. Manny explained it was the Hogendam Gap.

Manny and Johin had each earned a brass piece for helping to re-load a cart which had shed its crates of live chickens. Catching them all had taken two hours of terribly hot work. Johin secretly felt sorry for the poor animals, wishing she could let them go free.

Johin had wanted to spend the money on a really good piece of melon. Manny, annoyingly right as usual, said that there would probably be a dust storm, if not worse, that night, and they needed shelter and rest. The money bought them the right to a small patch of damp, rancid-smelling floor and a cup of water each in an isolated concrete bungalow with a corrugated metal roof. It stank and was alive with fleas.

The dust storm was terrible, and the threat of another earthquake had Manny holding his sides in pain. For long hours he rolled and thrashed about, trying to escape from the tearing inside himself. But morning came at last, and the dust subsided. Manny was weak and limp. Johin bathed his wound with water from the Pool. They ate breakfast from the satchel, and despite Johin pleading with Manny to rest longer, they set off.

Manny was very quiet. It was not just his usual 'listening' state, but a still, numb silence which brooded and hung about him as he stumbled along the road. He rested frequently. His feet were bleeding and the wound in the chest refused to heal. Large black flies laid long white eggs deep in Manny's flesh.

After a long session of picking at the eggs and maggots with a dry reed, Manny's chest was bleeding, and even he was reduced to whimpering. Johin threw down her tool of torture. 'Why aren't you getting better, Manny? Isn't the water from this Pool as strong as the other? I know you're going to be cross with me for saying this, but it looks almost as if the Lightwater isn't working this time. You're getting worse!'

Manny rolled over to look at her. He was very drawn and grey. 'It is all the same water. It is the Light within the water that matters. Water is water.' He spoke slowly and heavily. 'The Lightwater has not forgotten me. A long time ago, way back in the edges of the mists of Making, when Brilliance tore himself away from the Light, it was vowed that I should become as all creatures are, to heal them from the burning of his dazzling.

'What you call my "magic" is only the way things were *meant* to be. The fact that people die and suffer is only the effect of Brilliance shadowing us from the true Light.

'Brilliance will be Unmade, and then nothing will die or rot. When that happens, you will see that what you call "magic" is only what the Light calls "normal". But until the Unmaking is complete, there will be much suffering, as the shadow of Brilliance grows deeper and more foul every minute.'

Johin felt her heart sink. What if the magic of Brilliance was stronger than that of the Lightwater? It certainly looked like it. She said nothing because she did not want to frighten Manny when he was so ill.

Manny sat up painfully, and a crack appeared in the fragile crust on his wound. A fresh trail of blood and pus trickled slowly across his flaking skin.

Johin could not look. She peered along the empty road, shimmering hot and pink and purple in the noon-tide heat. She blinked back a tear. The heavy, quivering air made her feel light-headed.

'If you are from the River, how can Brilliance shadow you? How can he separate you from the River?'

Manny made her look at him. His blue-green eyes were pale and sunken. 'Trust me. I *am* the River, but I have become as human as you are. I must go through what you go through. That is the way it must be. But I am very weak and dry. My body will not last much longer, nor will our once lovely River Planet. The infection comes from the poison which is everywhere. It is very deep and very evil. We must hurry. Johin, help me, please . . .'

The need and grief in his face struck Johin so hard she could hardly breathe. Yet she could not look away. She was so empty and lost. If the River was so weak and vulnerable it could not help itself, what could *she* do?

She got to her feet, and with both hands pulled Manny upright.

'I can't carry you,' she said after a short struggle. 'You are heavier than when I first met you—or I am weaker.'

Manny was silent. His dry lungs were struggling for air. Johin propped him against her shoulder. His thin legs splayed behind him. His head lolled uselessly, and his arms swung limply.

'I can't carry you, Manny. Don't you understand? We're finished!'

Manny lifted his head. Suddenly, his muscles tightened. 'Oh no!' he moaned. 'Look!'

16
Hogendam

Johin turned her head slowly to see where Manny was staring.

Deep in the shaking yellow and purple haze of the distant mountains was a plume of dust. It came onwards, certain and steady. One plume separated into three. Black figures squatted like malignant flies at the base of each plume. A low droning noise became more persistent, and rose to a sharp hum.

Soon the huge silver hover bikes of the Water Guard patrol were pulling up beside Johin and Manny.

Neither of them could move. Manny's head hung loosely on Johin's shoulder. Johin stared in disbelief and horror.

Everything was over!

One of the Water Guards dismounted. She was a tall, thin Mud woman. Her hair was cut very short, and the black, loose-flapping bike suit made her look like a bird of prey as she peered down at the exhausted pair. Without taking her eyes off them, she shouted to her companions: 'I think we've got them!'

Menacingly, she manoeuvered her bike closer to Manny and Johin. 'Get on!' she snapped, with a sharp jerk of the head. 'You're under arrest!'

One of the other Guards dismounted, and helped to prise Manny away from Johin's shoulder.

'Have courage,' whispered Manny. 'The River has not

died yet. Keep singing.' And he was taken away.

Johin climbed stiffly up behind the woman, and watched with dismay, as Manny was strapped like luggage on to the back of a hoverbike.

'He'll be all right,' snapped the woman. 'You wouldn't want him to fall off, would you?' And with that, the bikes lifted, pitched, turned, and sped off towards Hogendam.

The cell was cold and almost dark. A jug of water and a plate with bread stood in the corner. They each had a straw mattress and a blanket.

Johin slept heavily. She dreamed her feet were set in concrete as Water Guards bore down on her like black vultures, flapping and calling in the night air. She could not run from the terror. She tried to call out, but could only make a faint gurgling and bubbling in her throat. Her chest pumped up and down, and the gurgling became rhythmical. Suddenly it became all-important, this strange sound that she was making.

Then her dream changed. She was seated on the ground, watching Manny's grey-covered form on the grass at Greenhevel. Everyone was looking at her, as she burbled and spluttered. She seemed to be ruining the beautiful singing of the Sand people—drowning it out with her cawing. She was scared she might ruin their healing magic, but she could not stop the noise!

Then, in her dream, she was alone. There was no one else to sing. *She* had to sing. She didn't know the words, but if she didn't sing, then all would be lost.

The line between Johin's dreaming and waking was very fine. She was still singing: strange words, with no meaning. It didn't matter what she sang, as long as she went on singing!

For hours she sat huddled under her blanket, singing softly. She watched Manny's limp form. Occasionally, he moved a little. He was still alive.

The sudden grating sound of a key in a lock made her angry. The singing was soothing and beautiful. She could not bear to stop it.

The Water Guard cadet was a girl of only a year or so older than herself. 'Get up. The Inspector wants you both.'

With a sinking feeling, Johin knew she must obey. Although the girl was unarmed and not very tall, she was better fed and stronger than they were. Neither she nor Manny could possibly get away from her.

Johin motioned towards Manny. 'My friend is very sick and cannot walk.'

The girl crossed the room, and turned him over with her foot. 'He's all right. He's had antibiotics and a good sleep. I don't know why they wasted medicine on a Sand boy, but it was the Inspector's orders.'

Manny, roused by the foot under his wounded shoulder, opened his eyes wide and gazed at the girl. She looked away quickly, avoiding his eyes.

'Get up!' she said curtly.

Manny pulled the blanket around his thin shoulders. His wound had a clean bandage. He winced as he stood up, and followed the girl without a word. Johin ran out of the room after them. She left Nuffle behind. He had found some little grey playmates, and was probably better off there, anyway.

They climbed a short flight of stairs, and found themselves in a concrete bungalow with ten rows of identical bunks.

'This must be the guardroom,' whispered Johin. Manny nodded, but followed the cadet in silence. They crossed a burning hot square. The ground hurt Manny's bare feet, and he danced painfully across the open area. Even Johin's feet burned through the soles of her sandals.

The heat seemed to be worse than she had ever known it. It was a devouring, cruel heat.

Eventually they stopped at another bungalow like all the rest: pinkish-yellow concrete, with darkened windows, all of which were firmly shut against sudden squalls of hot, sand-laden wind. The girl knocked at the blistering, black-painted door. A muffled voice answered. She opened the door, and pushed the prisoners in.

Inside, it was very dark. An armed guard nudged Johin and Manny through another door with the butt of his rifle. The door was slammed behind them.

Sitting framed against a small window, with his back to its burning light, was the bowed figure of the Inspector. Stabs of gold light glanced off highly polished shoulder buttons, as he dabbed at his face with a white handkerchief.

He made them sit facing the window, so the light caught them full in the face, but they could not see him. The sun hurt their eyes, but they tried to keep looking forward. After a long silence, a youngish voice said, 'You can come away from the window now. I see it is painful for you to sit there.'

'Thank you, Collim,' said Manny.

17

Hunger Mountain

The black shadow of a figure started, and the handkerchief was lowered. He moved slowly across the room and peered closely into the boy's face.

'How did you *know?*'

Manny returned his gaze. He smiled sadly.

Collim continued dabbing at his face. The handkerchief had not been just a disguise; it was a necessity. There was a red, running sore on his forehead.

Instead of the lively self-assured young man who had left Ardigham on the day of Manny and Johin's flight, here was a puffy, older face. Dark lines sat under his eyes, and he looked tired. Not from lack of sleep, but weary in a different way.

'I am glad it is you,' Collim said simply. 'I have had patrols out day and night looking for you. I was frightened that something awful might happen.'

'It just has,' said Johin sulkily. 'What are *you* doing here, anyway?'

'It wasn't my idea. The Chief arranged promotion for me, so I wouldn't get into trouble over my involvement with Manny and the Pool back at home. He thought I'd be better off out of the way. So now I'm an Inspector.' He spread his hands in a helpless gesture, and shrugged.

Johin peered into his face. 'You should have come with us, you know that, don't you?'

Collim nodded. 'Maybe, but how could I? I had work to

do. Things are never that easy when you're older. Anyway, are they treating you well?'

'As well as can be expected,' said Manny. 'Thank you for the medical treatment.'

Collim smiled. 'I had to bend the rules to get that. Medical care is not usually extended to Sand people. It's expensive.'

Manny bowed his thanks. 'I am very grateful.'

Johin could contain herself no longer. She jumped up from her chair, and grabbed Collim by the arms. The danger was too great for polite conversation. Their journey was urgent. Everything hung on their free-dom ... today, now!

'Collim, you have *got* to get us out of here. We *must* find the source, the River is dying! If you don't let us go immediately, then it may be the end of everything, and it'll be your fault!'

Collim looked at Johin's desperate face, and then at Manny's calm one.

'I suppose you're right. But like everything around here, it's easier said than done. I could find an excuse to let *you* go, Johin, but not Manny.'

'Why *not?*' demanded Johin. She was really angry now. She stood in front of her cousin, with her hands on her hips, and glared at him. 'Collim, look at me! I thought you *understood* about Manny and the River and everything ... I thought you were one of *us!* Don't you remember, Collim? The River, the Pool and what it all means? Don't give me that "I'm bigger than you and you're only a child" look. This is important! It's more important than a few rules. The whole future of the Planet is at risk! people's *lives* are at stake!

'*You* know that Manny isn't an ordinary Sand boy. Everything hangs on him being free. For once in your life, Collim, do something because you *know* it's right, not because you're scared of someone bigger than yourself!'

Collim winced and dabbed at his sore with his handkerchief, to avoid her penetrating eyes. He squirmed on his seat, then he sighed, and looked out of the window.

Over his shoulder, Johin and Manny could see a huge golden cone, which reached high into the sky. He pointed. 'Let me explain another way. Do you know what that is?'

Johin shook her head.

'That—is Heylebul Island.'

'What's that?'

'Don't you know what "Heylebul" means?'

Manny's voice almost chanted in her left ear: 'Heylebul means plenty. Enough for everyone and to spare for all comers...'

Collim winced again. 'It's the grain store. It's full to overflowing. Come, let's go for a walk. Drape yourself, Manny, I don't want you to be spotted.'

Manny covered himself as best he could with the stifling blanket.

Collim opened his office door and spoke to the guard. 'I'm taking these prisoners over to the Dam... I think the prospect of Genadatown may make them talk. Take any messages for me while I'm gone.'

'Yessir!' the guard snapped, saluting smartly.

Collim returned the salute and turned on his heel to walk between Manny and Johin.

They came to the edge of a deep, wide canyon. Heylebul Island rose steep and golden in the middle.

Fleets of hoverbikes whirred round it incessantly. Every few hundred strides there stood guardtowers, bristling with weapons and swathed in cruel barbed wire.

'I thought you said Heylebul meant enough for everybody?' asked Johin, staggered at the scene.

Collim shrugged. 'It does, and there is. But that's the way it's got to be. You see, we just can't take risks. The Sand people are in an ugly mood, and could attack us any day; even our own people are restive. The Wanderers have been making more and more daring raids. The situation is very, very dangerous.' He waved a hand at the guard towers. 'It costs a fortune to guard and patrol the Island every day. Fuel is very low for the hover bikes. But we must keep it up.'

Johin looked bemused. 'But you're being stupid again, Collim! It must be cheaper and easier just to distribute the food. If there's plenty, it ought to be shared.'

'Of course it would. Much cheaper. And much easier. It costs many times more to defend this pile than to grow more,' he laughed cynically. 'But as I keep telling you, things aren't that easy. There are two very important reasons for keeping things the way they are.

'Firstly, we don't know how long this drought may last, so we have to eke out supplies. Secondly, if we distribute the food, we will lose our hold on the people. We are keeping things together. Without the enforcement of the Drought Council's regulations there would be riots—even a war—and thousands of people would die needlessly. This is the price of peace.'

He motioned towards a long, cream-coloured wall which spanned the width and depth of the canyon where the two mountains met. 'That is Hogendam, the High Dam,' he said. 'Let's walk across it, and you will see what I mean.'

The light and heat were suffocating, and were magnified by the almost endless expanse of concrete. Feeling very tiny, high on top of the huge dam, Johin and Manny peered down into the arid depths of the river bed.

Collim waved his hand across the scene. 'Before the River died, this was an enormous hydro-electric dam. It also distributed water into the polders of Brotplain, off to your left, and to the higher reaches of the City, which is just out of sight, behind the hill on your right. Now, as you can see, it is nothing. Just a mockery of the wonderful achievements of the past.'

The sides of the canyon lay in massive layers of purple, pink and yellow rock, thrown together, one on top of the other—folded and dumped like a great unmade bed. It was magnificent as well as frightening. Once the River had filled the entire basin before them. Now it lay dry and empty.

Immediately in front of them was Heylebul Island. The steep sides of its rocky slopes were a huge bite out of the cliffs behind, and on top squatted the golden cone of the grain store. To their left were the low bungalows of Hogendam Camp, framed against the foothills of the mountains, behind which lay all Manny and Johin's adventures so far.

The foothills flattened smoothly into the distant green and gold levels, shimmering gently in the heat haze. 'That's Brotplain,' Collim explained. 'All the food is grown there. I'll show you that later. I think even you will be impressed.'

As they moved further along the dam wall, they could just see the edge of the City, the capital of that part of the Planet. It stood grey, crumbling and proud, at the base of the mountains. As at Ardigham, the River had once lapped its lower streets. It stood high and bare on a precipice now, teetering on the lip of the dry emptiness.

Between the Island and the City was a thin line of glistening silver. Johin stared at it for some moments before gasping, 'Is *that* the River? But it's so *low*. It's even worse than it was at home!'

Manny, who had stood silent for a long time, said quietly, 'It is almost gone. The time is very close. I am afraid Johin is right, Collim.' Then he pointed his thin, yellow arm to a pile of what looked like rubbish, flung recklessly on to the scree at the foot of the mountains as they joined the canyon. It lay discreetly out of sight of the City.

'What is that?'

Collim gulped and looked away. 'I had hoped you weren't going to ask that,' he said.

'I need to know,' insisted Manny.

'That is Genadatown.'

The word struck an icy chill in Johin's stomach, although she did not know why.

Collim looked carefully down at his sandals. 'As you know, "genada" is an old word for "grace" or "free gift". We are getting hundreds of Sand people drifting into Hogendam every week. They hear about Heylebul . . .'

'They call it "Hunger Mountain",' interrupted Manny.

' . . . So I've heard. Anyway, they come streaming in, claiming to be in need and expecting handouts. I *know* they're not evil, just hungry, but the official view is that by leaving their traditional way of life, they are intentionally making themselves destitute, and therefore they are turned away.'

'How cruel!' protested Johin. 'Can't you *do* something, Collim? You are an Inspector, after all.'

Collim looked at her rather sadly. 'I wish I could. There is no way I can help. It's the way things are and the way they must be. We can't just hand out free food and water to anyone who decides life here may be easier than in the desert. I know these Sand people have wonderful ways of coaxing water out of the most unlikely places. I've seen them do it. With due respect to you, Manny, they *are* lazy.'

Manny did not move. He just said quietly, 'But the water simply isn't there any more, Collim. There is nothing left to "coax".'

Collim swallowed and looked away.

'What happens to these people?' asked Johin urgently.

'For the most part, they are herded back into the hills. We can't let them stay here. There are more people than we can feed and care for as it is. Any who are fairly fit and strong are sent to Genadatown—as a an act of grace, pity, if you like. As you see, it is situated close to the River. It's better than the alternative.'

Manny peered down at the shanty town below. 'And then?'

'Our water pumps are short of fuel.'

'Fuel that could be saved if you stopped your wretched hoverbike patrol!' interrupted Johin angrily.

Collim ignored her. 'We turned the pumps off a very long time ago. The people of Genadatown earn their food, water and accommodation by carrying water up to Hogendam, Brotplain and the City.'

'By *hand?*' gasped Johin in horror.

'Yes,' mumbled Collim, who was feeling very uncomfortable. 'By hand.'

Manny stood tall, and held Collim in a steady gaze. Collim dabbed at the sore that had appeared where Manny's Mark had been. Hiding behind his handkerchief, he closed his eyes and tried to force away the unbidden memories of dying Sand babies.

'Why do you, of all people, let this go on?' Manny asked.

Collim refolded his handkerchief very carefully. 'It works. It keeps some of us alive.'

Johin was furious. Now she looked carefully, she could see a thin line of walkers trudging up from the valley floor. They were all bearing heavy yokes with canvas buckets. Women, children and men. It made no difference. They all slaved in the heat.

Collim led them back past Hogendam Camp to

Brotplain. He began to look very pleased with himself. 'This is the proof of the success of the way we work,' he said. 'Here we have a good area of land well irrigated, and planted with a modern, high-yield, low-moisture sustenance crop. The quality of this grain is excellent.'

Streams of pathetic workers, mostly Sand people, but with a few Mud people and Wanderers amongst them, pulled themselves wearily up the slope.

Suddenly Johin clutched at Manny's arm.

'Look!' she said. 'Look who's here!'

18
Genadatown

It was the King of the Wanderers. There was no doubt about it. His iron-grey hair was long and untidy, and his orange robe was torn and filthy. Around his ankle was a heavy manacle.

'How did he get here, Collim?' asked Manny.

'We pick up a few stronger workers at the slave markets,' Collim replied flatly, as if he were talking about chickens, not people. 'He was probably caught stealing or something.'

'But the Wanderers die if they stay in a town...' protested Johin.

Collim shrugged. 'They have their own special camp out on the hills. They are all right.'

Collim turned away from the scene. 'Do you mind if we go back now? I'm getting a raging headache. It ... it's the sun.'

Johin and Manny lingered for a few minutes. 'Is that what you meant by the River meeting the King on his own terms?' she whispered.

Manny nodded silently. He was watching the glistening water in the tiny channels and ditches which edged each little square field of growing grain. The water carriers all looked downcast and hopeless as they struggled up to the trough, emptied their buckets, turned and clambered down again.

A Water Guard caught sight of Manny and Johin. He

shouted, waving them away with his gun. They ran.

Manny caught Collim by the shoulder, and turned him so they could look face to face. 'That's where you are going to take me, isn't it? Genadatown.'

Collim nodded and walked on.

John's heart sank. She grabbed hold of Collim's arm. 'You can't!—Manny's got to be free! Everything depends on him, and you know it!'

'I'll do my best to set him free soon, but he won't stand a chance of escape here in Hogendam.'

'Then why capture us in the first place?' she challenged, wide-eyed.

'So I could protect you. I wanted to make sure you were both safe. From the condition you were in when they found you, I don't think you'd have made it on your own, so you should be grateful. I do care, honestly I do.'

'You call this "protection"?' raged John. 'Manny is so weak he'll *die* down there! Let him go—tonight, when it's dark!'

'I can't. It's too soon. Trust me. In a while they'll have forgotten about him, then we'll get him on his way.'

'But that'll be too late!'

Collim shrugged. 'It's the best I can do. If it wasn't for me, you'd both be dead.'

John glanced at Manny, huddled under the blanket. 'If he goes to Genadatown, so do I.'

'You don't have to, John, you can stay here with me,' said Collim. 'I can find an excuse.'

John looked at Manny and closed her eyes and thought of what she had seen. She shuddered, but the idea of staying with Collim and listening to his endless complacent excuses made her feel sick. 'No, I want to go. But I need to get Nuffle first.'

Collim shrugged. 'As you like. I'll have to send a Guard down with you. It won't look right if I go. By the way, this is yours, Manny.' He handed the Sand boy a soft green leather pouch.

Manny tossed it in his hand, and it clinked. 'What is it?'

'Gold. The Chief gave it to me for you the day you left, but what with Johin falling down the cliffs and you bringing her back like that . . . I don't know, it just went out of my head . . . I'm afraid it's not all there. I spent some of it on your medicine . . . and I bought myself a decent office, I'm afraid. You only get privilege the hard way around here.'

Manny looked at it. 'Will it buy food?'

'Yes, quite a lot.'

'Do that, and bring it down to Genadatown. While you're there, I'll treat that sore of yours.'

Johin pulled Collim aside and hurriedly whispered in his ear: 'What *did* happen the night Manny and I escaped from Ardigham? Manny just says I fell, and you said you would tell me one day. What did you mean when you said Manny "brought me back" like that? I get a funny feeling every time I think about it . . . but I need to know!'

Collim looked at her out of the corner of his eye, then hung his head. 'The Mayor's dog chased you, and you fell over the cliff top.'

'But I can't have, that would have killed me . . .' her voice trailed off.

Collim's dark skin was dull and damp. He looked at her as if he was scared. He nodded. 'Yes.'

Within the hour, Collim stood alone and unmoving in his stifling office. Once again he was left holding the little leather bag as he watched Johin and Manny walk out of sight. This time, they were under armed guard.

The tall, sour-looking Water Guard pushed open several doors with the butt of his rifle, until he found what he was looking for: a thin, shivering old man crouching terrified in the darkened corner of a tumbledown shack.

'Out, you!' he ordered. 'Grace is up!'

The old man was tiny and pathetic. He pulled himself painfully into the light. He blinked accusingly at Manny and Johin, and stumbled away. Johin and Manny were shoved inside.

'There you stay. Work starts at dawn.'

'You didn't have to throw him out because of us,' Johin protested. 'We don't mind sharing!'

'Good!' was all he said, as he turned on his heel and marched out of the town.

As their eyes grew used to the dim light of the hovel, they saw there were blankets, bottles and a few pots spread around.

'It looks like we shall be sharing anyway,' said Manny. 'I'd say two or three families live here.'

Johin caught her breath. 'Two or three *families?* Don't you mean people?'

Manny shook his head. 'I wish I did.' They cleared a space big enough for them both, and tried to make themselves comfortable.

'What do you think will happen to him?' Johin asked.

'He'll go to the city dump,' came a thin voice from the corner. For the first time they saw a woman huddled in the deep shadows. She was clutching a baby. 'Please, can you spare me a little water?' she said.

Manny went over to her and handed her the leather bottle. 'How old is your baby?' he said gently, touching the tiny head.

'A year'.

'But he's so tiny, how could he be a year old?' asked Johin, stunned.

'We are hungry, and thirsty,' she replied. 'Our children do not thrive.'

Manny looked around in the stinking dark. 'Do you have a cup? I'll pour some for your child.'

'He's too weak to drink. I'm trying to give my own milk, but I am so dry now . . . I think we will be the next to go to the dump.'

'What is this dump?' asked Manny, pressing the water bottle into her hands again.

'When we are not strong enough to work any longer, they throw us out. There is nowhere else to go other than the dump. It is at the top of the scree behind us, and in a dip between the hills. The rubbish from the City is brought there every day.

'There is sometimes enough to keep us alive, but it is dangerous. The ground shifts, and the food scraps are rotten. When we are of no use here any more, we fight for survival up there, until we drop dead.

'The only good thing about it is that it is fairly near the source of the River, and there are a few muddy puddles and springs of water. Some have survived there for months, even a year.' She shrugged. 'It is usually disease that gets us in the end.'

Manny took a drink and passed the bottle to Johin.

'We had better get some rest if we have to start early tomorrow.' He handed round the last of the supplies from his satchel and curled up in a corner.

At dusk, the workers returned, sweating and weak. Each had a small black loaf and a tin mug of water. Johin watched a thin young man go to the woman in the corner and offer her his rations. She said something and nodded towards Johin and Manny. The man turned and smiled, held out his hands in greeting, and gratefully ate his full ration.

They were woken early, by a Water Guard slamming the side of the hut with a rod. The noise was painful, and the flimsy walls wobbled drunkenly under the blows.

Shouts and moans and children crying bombarded Manny's ears. He sat up wide-eyed. His voice shook. He sounded scared. 'It's close, Johin. I can feel it.'

'What is?' muttered Johin as they staggered outside. She never heard his reply, as hundreds of famished, weary labourers swept them apart.

Eventually, they came to several long tables where they were given one drink, from a bowl of stale, cloudy water, and a small black loaf each. When they had eaten and drunk, the people were divided into groups and set to work.

Johin, because she was fresh and comparatively strong, was given a heavy wooden yoke. It was half as long as she was tall, and carved in a hollow curve, with a deep piece cut out to fit around her neck. Her task was to collect full buckets from a slippery step at the water's edge, where the children filled empty buckets from the River and clipped them back onto the yokes.

Then Johin crossed a rickety bridge over the River, now scarcely a stream, and started the steep cliff climb up to Hogendam. The buckets were too heavy for her. She was terrified of spilling a drop, as tall, brutal-looking overseers stood every few paces to encourage any laggers with whips. She wished Manny were there.

They were allowed one scoop from the water dipper each climb. If the barrel was empty, there was no waiting for it to be filled. One had to wait until next time, or the time after that.

She had begun determined not to be beaten. She had sung heartily, but not one of the Sand people around her joined in as she had thought they would. During the long day, her voice became lower and lower, until she was silent. It was difficult to climb and sing, after all. By the time the evening came, her shoulders were bleeding, her lips were swollen and cracked from thirst, and she felt dizzy and light-headed.

Weariness hit her like the blast of a sandstorm, and she was soon asleep. She woke with the gentle sensation of having her shoulders bathed by Manny, who sat smiling next to her.

'Better?' he said simply.

Johin nodded and sat up.

'Would you like me to do your shoulders now?'

'Thanks, but Mara here has bathed them already.' He motioned to the tired mother they had helped the night before.

Johin bit her lip. The old jealousy that anyone should do anything for *her* special friend, was gnawing at her again. She mustn't let it get at her this time. She nodded and said, 'Good, I'm glad. Thank you, Mara.'

'Collim is here,' whispered Manny. 'Come outside.'

There in the shadows, dressed in the plain white uniform of an ordinary Water Guard, was Collim. He was sweating with the effort of carrying a large bag of flour all the way down from Hogendam.

'It was a bit of an effort getting here unseen,' he said. 'I had to pretend to be relieving the night patrol. How I got here without being challenged about the sack, I don't know.'

Collim puffed and dabbed at his forehead, especially around the sore. 'I suppose you couldn't ...? I mean you did promise ...'

'Of course,' said Manny kindly, and he dived back into the steeply leaning hut for his water bottle.

Johin turned and confronted Collim squarely. 'Listen, it's awful here. You've got to do something! Innocent people are dying ...'

Collim shrugged. 'I don't see what I *can* do. People are dying everywhere. At least this way some of us get fed.

Some of us will survive. If we stop what's happening here, if we break Heylebul open, maybe none of us will last. It's a gamble, it's hard, but it's the only way, Johin, believe me. I'll try to get you two away from here soon, I promise, but there's really nothing I can do for these others. Anyway, as you're so fond of telling me, the River will look after them.'

'But can't you *see*, the River has given *us* the responsibility of changing things!'

Collim raised his eyebrows and looked resigned. 'In that case, I wish the River would hurry up and give us the *means* to do something, as well the responsibility. It's very unfair telling me to *do* something, when it's all so big and beyond my power.'

'Hold still,' said Manny, who had been quietly listening in the shadows. 'This may sting a little.'

19
The River Plays Fair

Johin didn't know whether to laugh or cry.

The small, sturdy donkey was magnificent. His coat was rich brown, and his big eyes were deep and dark. Collim took a step backwards and tried to say, 'stop it, what are you all laughing at . . .?' but it came out as 'eeerh, igh eeeor!'

Collim stopped and looked down. His neat grey hooves were well trimmed, but the Water Guard's uniform pulled tightly around his stomach, digging deeply into his new girth.

'No, no!' he exclaimed in horror. 'Egh, egh, ooogh! . . . I don't believe it..! Eeeegh hoor!'

Manny laid a gentle hand on the thick, bristling mane. 'There, old friend. You'll find that sore healing well by the morning. Now, get some rest. Be grateful. The River has given you the means of helping to ease the poverty and hardship here, just like you said it ought to.'

Morning light saw a very sorrowful little donkey indeed. The night had been chilly, and he had lost his uniform to a crowd of giggling Sand women.

They had unpicked the Water Guard insignia, and by dawn, the garments were altered to give new breeches and a fresh tunic to labourers who had been nearly naked in their rags.

The Water Guards looked surprised to see the donkey. No one could remember seeing it arrive. They tried to lead it up to Hogendam where it could be put to use, and save the cadets a job or two. But it would not go. However much they beat it, kicked it, tempted it: it would not leave Genadatown.

At last an inspector came down to see what was happening. He shrugged. 'It may as well work for us here as up there. Keep it well fed.'

'Well fed' in Collim's terms was not what the Water Guards had in mind. By the end of a day's toil, sweating up steep stony slopes with huge panniers of water, he was sore, tired, weak and very hungry.

After work, Manny caught the donkey and whispered in his ear. 'You wanted to know what you could do to help—now I have a few little jobs for you.' He took Collim to a hut which was twisting and falling over so dangerously it was scarcely still standing. Collim's broad rump was ignominiously backed against the flimsy wall of the house. With a thick stick to encourage him, he was made to push and push until the hut was upright again.

He was left there for what seemed like hours, supporting the whole weight of the hut on his backside, while men pushed poles and rocks against the sagging wall to keep it firm. He was most unhappy.

At last, exhausted and sore, Collim turned to go back to his own shed to rest. But Manny had other ideas. A firm hand on his bridle steered him towards another hut. While they walked, a quiet voice whispered, 'How's the sore on the face, Collim?'

Collim could not reply. He stood helpless while he was loaded up with a few possessions, a woman and two babies. They were hoping to flee Genadatown and be well on the road to Greenhevel before dawn. They knew that if they stayed, they would be thrown out to the dump.

Collim walked and walked. His passengers were a

backbreaking load, pitifully thin though they were. In the middle of the night, a small group of Wanderers met them and, taking the exhausted family onto their camels, promised to deliver them to Greenhevel. Collim let the weary Manny climb onto his back, and trudged back to Genadatown.

By dawn, Collim had not slept at all. His hooves were bleeding, and he could hardly lift his large bony head.

For two more exhausting days, Collim laboured until his shoulders were raw with the weight of the panniers. The rough hemp straps cut cruelly into his flesh. In the evenings, after a short rest, Manny would set Collim to work again, pulling, heaving and carrying for the people of Genadatown.

At first, Collim was furious at the trick that Manny had played on him. A donkey! Him, the Water Guard Inspector! But secretly, deep inside, he knew he had been warned. He knew he deserved it, and he had only been given what he had demanded—fair play from the River. Now he had not only the responsibility for the Sand people, but also the means to help them.

Collim understood what was happening. He had seen Manny's magic before. He knew that he would be all right, unlike the poor, helpless, cruelly-treated people he was working among. He worked with a will. He had no right to complain. Besides, as Manny promised, the sore was healing up nicely.

On the third day, the River was only a weak trickle. Here and there were small pools. Where the water had been waist-deep two days ago, and thigh-deep yesterday, it was now scarcely wet.

Manny was very weak. 'It is almost time now,' he had whispered to Johin, as they separated that morning.

During the heat of the day, Manny collapsed.

In the distance was the rumbling of a threatened earthquake. Manny sprawled on the shingle of the River-bed, like an empty pile of tattered clothing.

The Water Guard on duty kicked him and threatened him. His cruel whip licked around Manny's legs and back. Still Manny didn't move.

The Guard called for the donkey. 'This one's a goner. Load him up and take him out to the dump!' Manny was tied on like a sack—bound hand and foot under the donkey's stomach. His balding head bounced up and down as the donkey swayed, picking a careful way over the rocks.

Johin was high up the canyon side when it happened. Suddenly, something made her stop and look round. 'Manny!'

She *had* to follow.

Now.

She had no way of knowing whether that limp bundle slung over Collim's back really was Manny, but even if it wasn't, she had to go. But how? She was only half-way up the cliff face with full buckets. At this rate, it could take another half hour or so before she had emptied her buckets at the top, and climbed back down again.

That would all take too long. She would have to think of a way of escaping from the overseer's scrutiny.

Johin looked down. It was a long drop. The pathway up the cliff face was well cut, and wide enough to walk on comfortably, but a feigned fall could end in death. A little further up was a small passing platform. There, she could fall and twist her ankle reasonably safely. If she looked convincingly injured, she would get dismissed; without food—but she would be free.

Just as she was gazing upwards trying to perfect her plan, she missed her footing, and really did fall. The path, made slippery with splashes of water, just seemed to slide from under her feet. The world turned upside down, and she screamed.

Slowly, painfully slowly, she watched her yoke and buckets toss and tumble all the way down. The fall seemed to take ages. Cool, silver streams of water poured and sparkled in the sunlight as the buckets spilled all down the cliff face.

Suddenly, she realized that *she* had stopped falling. Something had her fast, although her arms and one leg were flailing in the air.

Long, strong arms pulled her upright. She froze. It was a face she recognized, and had never wanted to see again. His teeth were rotting, and his orange robe was shredded and torn, but he still had that iron-grey hair and fierce look. It was the Wanderer King.

The heavy iron shackles on his wrist hurt her as he hauled her upright. But she was alive.

She looked at him, terrified, but grateful.

'Thanks,' she said shakily.

The man screwed up his dark, ugly face and laughed. He smelled putrid and foul. 'We meet again. Only, it seems, it was me who went to the slave market, not you!'

He put Johin back on her feet, picked up his buckets and trudged on up the path.

Trembling, Johin held out her hands and said, 'Thank you. May the River meet you on your own terms.' It just seemed to be the right thing to say.

The overseer of that section had been watching the whole scene. All at once, he thundered down, roaring at Johin to go and retrieve her buckets, prodding her with his rifle to make the point.

Limping badly, Johin obeyed, picking her way carefully down the rocky path.

At the bottom, she collected her gear, and returned across the bridge. The Water Guards were in the middle of some sort of heated row, and did not notice when she slipped away from the River, back to her hut.

In the cool, stagnant dark, she rubbed her aching limbs and called Nuffle. She gathered the empty food satchel and the water bottle, slipped out of the hut, and wound her way through the ramshackle streets, up the scree, and into the open.

20
Shams and Imitations

The scree slope was high, dangerous and loose. The stones, which had never been smoothed by water, were painfully sharp. Johin turned her ankle many times, and often fell, cutting her hands and feet badly. She put Nuffle into the satchel so she could use both hands to climb.

She tried to keep her weight above her feet, and that helped to stop the sliding. Once or twice she thought of turning away from the scree to follow the road. But that was longer and slower, with a greater risk of being caught.

She kept thinking about how low the River was ... just the odd little shaking and dimpling of water in the pools, showing where a thin trickle was still flowing. In her mind's eye she thought of Manny, slung as dead over Collim's donkey back. She must keep going!

Suddenly, she realized she had reached the top of the scree, and a smoother slope faced her. Ahead, there was a sort of a saddle in between the hills. She had seen the Water Guard lead Collim and Manny that way, she was sure.

Once she had left the scree and the outcrop from which it had fallen, the slopes became high and rounded. It was more difficult to climb because the ground was so bare and hard; her feet often slid. It felt like climbing glass. Collim must have struggled here, she thought, especially with Manny to carry.

She was exhausted when she reached the top. In the hollow below was the dump. It was huge—easily as big as Heylebul Island; literally a mountain of fly-blown rubbish, animal corpses and rotting food. From where she stood, the sweet stench of decay wafted up to her on a breeze.

It was a shrine to uselessness. Even the people were useless. A small knot of stick-like Sand people were going about their few daily tasks. There was no hope of life or dignity left. This was the end.

Then she spotted Collim and Manny. Johin flattened herself on the bare earth and peered down the slope.

The Water Guard had dumped Manny on the ground, and was now tugging at Collim's halter with all his might. Collim, however, was, as Manny had always promised, an extremely good donkey. He worked hard, but he could also be quite stubborn. And he was being stubborn now.

The Water Guard was struggling with all his might to get Collim to return to Genadatown with him. Collim was having none of it. He kicked and butted, and eventually he bit the poor man so hard, he ran howling back down the road to safety. Left in peace at last, Collim nosed Manny over onto his back, and began to lick the boy's face. Tears streamed down the donkey's long brown nose.

The elderly Sand man who had been thrown out of the hut for Johin and Collim appeared slowly and cautiously from behind a shack. He came softly up to Collim, offering a handful of grass while reaching for Collim's head with his free hand. He obviously had ideas about the usefulness of a donkey on the dump. Collim took the grass gladly, but shied when the man grabbed for his halter. His hooves caught the old man on the legs and hands. The man cursed and swore, but he would not give up.

Johin was fascinated by the sight of the old man dancing around Collim, trying to coax and cajoul him closer, but when he grabbed an iron chair leg and advanced on Collim, she stood up.

'I don't think you'll get the donkey to come with you like that,' she said quietly. 'But he will follow *me*, if you help me get that boy on the donkey's back again, and take us to shelter.'

The man looked at her suspiciously. 'You're the couple that had me turned out of my hut. I suppose you've come to throw me out of *here* now!'

Johin smiled, spreading her hands open in the Sand people's greeting. 'My name is Johin. I have come to help my friend here. We mean you no harm. We never did. We just need rest for the night, then we will be on our way.'

The man sniffed and looked sideways at them. 'Since when has one of the Mud people ever not meant harm to me?' and he spat over his shoulder.

Johin looked steadily at him. 'If you need the donkey, he will help you, but that is the only way you will get him to come.'

The old man sniffed again. 'Well, I suppose you'd better come then. M'name's Pit. Let's get the boy buried first. We don't put them on the dump . . . it's not right. I've got a pickaxe and shovel.'

Johin touched Manny's back. There was still a flicker of life. 'I don't think he's dead yet. He can't be.'

Pit shrugged. 'It won't be long. I'm not wasting good water on him, if that's what you think.'

'It's all right, I have my own,' she said.

Between them they heaved Manny's long, thin, yellow body onto Collim's back, and picked their way through the rubbish to a hut made of planks and sticks, covered with rags, and plastered with cracked earth.

It stank even worse than the hut in Genadatown. A few

pitiably thin women with sickly children were there, with two or three older people. Hunger and thirst made them look ancient. Huge, black flies crawled everywhere.

Johin gave Manny water from the Pool, and he recovered a little, but she could not get him to eat. Their hosts offered putrid scraps from the dump, green and maggot-laden. Johin decided to go without. Nuffle scavenged some grass seeds. How he managed to get so fat on so little amazed Johin.

Collim was put to graze by one of the many muddy puddles edged with thin grass which were dotted around the dump.

'I never imagined the dump could be so huge,' said Johin in disgust.

Pit waved a hand towards the rubbish. 'It's said that it used to stand even higher, but since the earthquakes, the ground below has collapsed. It's all fallen into some kind of underground fault,' he said.

Suddenly, Johin remembered that the source of the River was said to be nearby.

Pit shook his head and laughed toothlessly. 'The source? Come on, I've nothing better to do. I'll show you where it is. You'll get no joy though!'

Intrigued, Johin left Manny where he was. The air was still and heavy, and the distant rumbling foretold yet another earthquake. It would be a long, painful night. Manny would need all the strength and sleep he could get.

She stopped to tell him where she was going. He nodded weakly.

An hour's trudge over the hills and twisting down through a smooth, empty valley, brought them suddenly into a stark landscape. The rocks were pink, purple and yellow, like everywhere else, but scored across the plain was a shallow, twisting canyon.

Every few hundred strides was a little shack, giving shade to the Water Guards against the relentless sun. Peering out from the shelters were long rifle barrels, glinting in the sunlight.

The old man laughed in a mad, heat-crazed way. 'There you are, all the water in the Planet, and not a drop for us.'

The valley had a few stunted drought trees, and rough grass and weeds grew along what had been the River bed.

The thin trickle swung round to their right. Pit told her it skirted the mountain on which the City was built, then it turned back in a great loop to flow past Heylebul Island and Hogendam.

The old man straightened himself. 'I'm off!' he announced suddenly. 'It doesn't do to hang around here. We can be shot on sight . . . or worse.'

'What can they do to you, other than send you back to Genadatown?'

The old man looked at her sideways. 'That's for the fit ones,' he said, and trudged off.

Johin knew she had to be quick. She guessed Pit would not do anything for Manny. To him, Manny was only a waste of energy and water. She suspected that the old man might even put an end to him, in the hopes of getting Manny's water ration.

But she had to find the source. Far below, the tiny trickle of water was only an intermittent glimmer in the sun. Time was very short.

She started to climb carefully down into the valley. She was so tired and hungry, she was almost past being frightened. She took Nuffle out of her pocket and put him on her shoulder, as she always did when she was needing company.

Every few paces she would lie still and hope that her movement would not be spotted. There would be nowhere to hide if shooting started. The sharp stones hurt her stomach. Her tunic was ripped and her head ached. Slowly and painfully she made her way downwards, until she found a point where she could see the River emerging.

Where the hills met the plain, cracks and caves yawned. One looked like a wide, singing mouth, worn into shape by thousands of years of rushing water. Once, the gushing River had filled the mouth, every second of every day. Johin just could not imagine that much water. It was beyond her understanding, yet she could see it had been true.

Stretched across the mouth of this gigantic cave was a forest of barbed wire overlooked by a guardhouse. It was going to be impossible. They had come all this way for nothing. There was no way Manny could climb unseen down here, let alone crawl through those defences. She sobbed dry tears until she slept.

When she woke, she was lying with the burning heat of the sun on her back. Nuffle was munching on a piece of wild grass (he really was getting terribly fat). She felt as if she had been drifting.

There was a figure looking down at her. She sat up and sheltered her eyes.

'Manny?'

He held his hand out to her. 'Hurry, Johin, get out. Quickly. It isn't safe here. I've found the source, and done everything I need to do. Now move! There's going to be another earthquake!'

Johin stood up, stiff from lying on the ground for so long.

She pushed her hair back and looked at Manny, 'But how did you ... I mean you were almost dead when I left you ...'

Manny wasn't looking at her; he was peering up into the hills. 'I have powers you don't know about. Anyway, it's all over now. Come *on*, Johin.'

'Just a minute. I've got to get Nuffle.'

Manny scowled irritably. 'Oh bother that wretched mouse! Come *on!*'

She looked hard at him. 'What's happened to you, Manny? You're not the same.'

'I'm tired, that's all. Do hurry.'

'I'm not going without Nuffle!' she insisted, feeling very hot and angry. 'How can you be so horrid, Manny? You've never been like this before!'

From the corner of her eye she saw Nuffle hiding behind a stone. She crouched down and called him. 'Come on, you silly animal, it's only us.' When she moved forward, Nuffle moved back.

Manny clicked his tongue impatiently and dived to grab the mouse. It squeaked and crawled into a deep crack, where even Manny's slender hand could not reach. 'Oh, we'll have to leave the stupid thing!' he snarled, and grabbing Johin's wrist, he tugged her away.

Somthing snapped inside Johin. She pulled back at his hand and swung Manny round to face her. Looking straight into his eyes she saw something she recognized. 'You're not Manny!' she challenged. 'Nuffle loves Manny, but he's terrified of you! You're Brilliance; I can see it in your eyes. You're just a sham!'

In a flicker of light the figure gave a spine-chilling leer, and vanished.

Johin found herself rooted to the spot. She could not believe what had happened. To have confronted a rock fall that looked like Brilliance was one thing, but to have stood up to him face to face, that was terrifying! She stood there, unable to move, shivering despite the heat. The feeling of evil was still everywhere, strangling and threatening.

Nibbling at her toes was an angry little Nuffle. She picked him up and looked into his perfect ruby eyes. 'You knew, didn't you, Nuffle my love? Come on, let's get

Manny. We must be very near the end now.'

On the top of the slope where the hills met, was a fat, black silhouette. It was the donkey-Collim, carrying the real Manny, slowly picking a way down the slope. Manny was clinging on for dear life, as he swayed weakly on Collim's broad back.

She rushed up to meet them. 'Oh Manny, thank goodness!' she said, giving him a hug. 'Brilliance is here!'

Manny smiled at Johin. 'I know. You did well. The River is growing strong within you.' With a sigh, Manny pulled himself upright. 'I am very weak, and I need strength. I must bathe in the River before I can go on.'

Johin stopped dead. 'You *can't*, Manny. It's awful! There are armed guards everywhere. They'll kill us as soon as look at us.'

Manny pushed himself into a sitting position. He stretched out his arms as if he would embrace the whole valley. Filling his bony chest with air he sang a soft, low song, which soothed even the scorching heat. Johin struggled to stop her head nodding. She jerked her eyes open as the last soft notes faded.

'They will not see us now.' he said. Slowly they scrambled down the valley slopes to the dry River bed. The thin trickle of water was scarcely ankle-deep.

Johin kept looking around, expecting to see Water Guards come running out, shouting and shooting. But the dead silence of the late afternoon was broken only by screaming vultures overhead.

Manny had turned Collim's head upstream, and there, against the barbed wire at the base of the cave, was a pool, deep enough to bathe in. Johin pulled Manny gingerly off the donkey, and helped him to the water's edge. Collim bowed his head and drank.

'Come,' Manny said. 'We are travel-stained and very weary. We have been through so much. I want you to dip

159

me in the pool. Right under. I must be reunited with the River once more.'

Johin knew better than to argue.

It was icy—colder than anything she had ever experienced before. As she lowered herself into the water, the cold hit her so hard that she gasped in pain. She could not breathe. Manny shivered, and held on tightly to Johin's arm.

Slowly, she made sure she had a good grip of his skinny body, as it floated and bobbed on the black, mirrored surface of the pool. She stepped out, one foot at a time, terrified lest her foot should slip, or that the bottom of the pool might suddenly fall away below her.

Manny breathed deeply. His body was no more than a mere bundle of sticks. His eyes were so tired and sunken, his face so dry and dust-streaked—poor Manny! Johin swallowed the lump that had suddenly come into her throat. He was such a good, kind person. It was all wrong that things should end like this!

Suddenly she blurted out: 'Let me take you home. Mum and Dad will nurse you back to health, then perhaps you can try again. Wouldn't you like to live quietly at home with us for a bit? Why don't you make the Pool of Making produce enough water to restore the Planet? I'm sure you could!'

Manny's sad eyes shut slowly. He leaned back and submerged himself into the unseen depths.

Johin was left hugging her words and wishing she had never said them. She knew they were not true. What she had asked for was a patching-up job . . . an imitation of the truth, something that did not hurt too much. It would solve nothing. It was Brilliance again, distracting, offering a cheap ride, when nothing but the terrible Magic of Unmaking would do.

Suddenly Manny's wet face, shining with light on

water, appeared in front of her. 'Come on!' he urged with something of his old cheeky grin. 'The water's lovely!'

He took her hand firmly and pulled her down.

She had never swum in her life; she had never been under water before, except that night at Ardigham, and then she had ... she had known nothing about it.

There was no need to breathe. Manny pulled her, floating coolly through time, into the depths of life itself, depths untouched since the Planet was made.

She could hear the words of his mind. He was not speaking. 'Come, and let the River flow over you, let every part of you be washed. Let the dust and weariness and pain float away, give it up to the River. Be in the River, let it be in you. Be one with the Lightwater.'

Slowly and gracefully they swam back towards the surface. The green shimmering light shook, and was broken by a large black shape floating on the surface. Bigger and bigger it grew, until Collim's head and neck stretched down to touch them.

Laughing, Manny broke the surface and caught hold of Collim's ridiculously long ears. 'Very well, my friend, you too!' and he guided the dusty brown donkey until he stood with only his muzzle and ears above the water. 'Hold your breath' he said, playfully plunging the animal all the way down.

The three of them spluttered to the surface, laughing and cold, splashing each other as if they were on a picnic.

Manny breathed deeply and looked around. 'Well, here goes,' he said. This really is it!'

He pulled himself out of the water and sat on a shining black rock. He smiled gently. 'I can walk now, at least. If you want to go back, don't feel badly about it. You have come as far as anybody could.'

1But Johin wasn't listening. 'Nuffle? Where's Nuffle?' she said.

21
The Depths of Darkness

Collim clambered out of the pool, his hooves slipping and catching on the wet stones. He offered a hoof to Johin who was scrambling after him.

'This way,' she shouted, grabbing the water bottle as she ran. 'I think Collim's seen Nuffle!' Without stopping for her sandals, Johin ran painfully up the hillside after the donkey. A whisk of a long pink tail betrayed a ball of creamy white fur disappearing into a small crack in the hillside.

Manny caught up, panting. His bathe in his beloved River had given him new strength and life.

'I think I could just squeeze in,' said Johin. 'Could you wait, please? I know what you have to do is more important, and I will come with you, but I can't go without Nuffle!' Manny didn't hesitate.

'Of course you must find him. Where is he? Can you see?'

'No, it's too dark in here.'

'Hold on,' he said, and scrambled back down towards the dry river bed. He gathered a long bundle of dry reeds, and plaited them into a pole the length of his own forearm, then, with two flints he struck a spark and caught the ends of the reeds alight. They began to smoulder with a red glow and a sweet smell.

'I'm coming,' he said.

Manny turned sideways and slid his thin body through

the crack. Collim pushed his nose in too, but he got stuck at the shoulders. However much he heaved and twisted his rump, which waved and skidded in the air outside, he could go no further.

Manny turned and patted him on the nose. 'Sorry, old chum. Our ways part here. Go and see what you can do for the Sand people at the dump. Wait for me there, oh, and find yourself some clothes, you'll be needing them soon.' Manny gave the sad donkey a hug, and once again traced the shape of the Mark in the wide, brown head, making a shiny path in the wet hair.

'We'll start again now, my friend,' the boy said softly, and he turned to follow Johin.

The narrow cave they found themselves in was little more than a slit between two slabs of rock. There was no floor, they had to wedge their feet against the sides, grazing their toes and heels painfully.

'I'm sure he's ahead, I can hear him squeaking and rustling,' whispered Johin. 'He's running away from me. I wish he'd stop!'

Manny squeezed past Johin. There was just enough light to catch a gleam of a white furry shape scurrying up and down ahead of them.

Manny followed a little way. 'I think your mouse knows a thing or two we don't,' he announced,

'What do you mean?' Johin demanded, slipping and scraping her leg as she did so.

'I think this way may lead down to the River's underground tunnel,' he said. 'When we were in the pool, I dived below the barbed wire to see if we could get in that way, but the Water Guards have done their job too thoroughly. I did not want to use all my strength undoing the wire. I knew we would have to look for another way in. Now it seems as if your Nuffle may have found it for us. *This* way will rejoin the main channel fairly quickly. It is going in the right direction.'

Johin wedged her hands and feet across the gap. 'And if it doesn't?'

Manny thought for a few seconds. As the tunnel took a sudden dip, he caught his head on an over-hanging piece of rock. 'Ow! If it doesn't, I don't know what will happen.'

'You don't think this is another of Brilliance's tricks to distract us? Hey, hold that torch up will you? I can't see a thing.'

'No, it doesn't feel evil, and Nuffle wouldn't be running towards it if it were. He has a very wholesome instinct for what is good.'

'True, especially if it is edible. But couldn't he be enchanted or something?'

'Not Nuffle. He knows, or smells something we don't. Look!' Manny stopped suddenly, and Johin, who could see nothing in the deep enveloping blackness, thumped straight into Manny, who dropped the torch.

'Mind out! Look, here it opens out into a cave with a proper floor. Can you feel the rippling shapes underfoot? This has had water in it for thousands of years. Once it must have been part of an old water course.'

'Yes, but *which* one?' asked Johin glumly.

Manny picked up the torch, blew on it gently to increase its light, and held it high. Johin gasped. High above them stretched an enormous cavern. Hanging down from the roof, long and cold, were huge grasping fingers of living rock. These massive stalactites met pointed teeth of stalagmites below. The cave floor flowed in ripples, slowly deepening into the mountain's roots. She felt as if she were standing in the jaws of a terrible monster. Vivid green and red streaks trickled down the yellow stone of the wall like blood.

Manny held her hand. 'Don't worry, they're just rocks.'

'But they are bleeding!'

'No, they're not,' he reassured her. 'The red is iron, and the green is copper. Didn't you know that metals come from the ground?'

'I suppose I did,' she answered. 'I just never dreamed it would be like this.'

Manny searched with his dull little torch, until he caught sight of the tiny fleck of white which was Nuffle, scurrying across the slippery cave floor with great speed. It was all that Manny and Johin could do to keep up with him. Suddenly he disappeared.

'Nuffle? Nuffle!' called Johin in sheer panic. 'Where are you?'

Their echoes caught the deep shapes of the cavern, tumbling around the stony emptiness. Then there was silence. Johin felt suddenly how deep inside the mountain they were. She wished that someone could cut the side of the hill open and lift her out. She was caught in the bowels of the Planet. Would she ever be free again? Half of her felt that if only Nuffle were there, then everything would be all right. The other half of her wanted to run berserk, screaming through the empty caverns, until the daylight found her.

Manny sensed her fear and held her hand tightly. 'Not far now,' he said reassuringly. 'Listen!'

At first Johin could hear only their own heavy breathing and the tiny scratching of Nuffle's claws, then a plop, plop, drip, splash! echoed more and more loudly.

'There's Nuffle,' said Manny bounding forwards. 'And do you see that trickle? That's the River!'

In his excitement, Manny let go of Johin's hand. She screamed: 'I can't stand this, let me out!'

The glimmering red glow of the torch came back towards her, and Manny's thin hand searched for hers. 'Here I am. It's all right.'

Just then, thousands of sharp jabs of light appeared in

front of them. They were of every colour, but all small and sharp. Faster and faster they moved, glancing and shifting in a fearful dance all around. Manny and Johin stood back to back and the strange dancers closed in on them. 'Close your eyes!' ordered Manny. 'It's not real!'

'It *is* real, I assure you, my little man!' hissed a voice, very near to Johin's left shoulder.

'Very real!' sang the voice, near her right shoulder now. Round and round the voices span, taunting her to open her eyes and see how very real and pretty the lights were. Dazzling balls of brightness filled the cave, whirling and spinning around her head until she did not know whether she was upright or upside down. Her eyes were tightly closed, but they could not keep out the lights . . . Slowly her legs sagged under her, and she lay on the floor, staring at the giddy dance. Every ball of light bore Brilliance's face. The evil was squashing them again.

'Close your eyes and think of real Light!' ordered Manny. 'Think of sunshine. Think of the River. Think of the taste of the Pool of Making. Sing, Johin! Sing the Song!'

Weakly Johin tried. The meagre squeak she managed sounded silly, but, following Manny's clear voice, she kept going. With her eyes closed, and singing as loudly as she could, she found she could stand again. Not daring to open her eyes, she held her hand out for Manny. He caught it and pulled her firmly out of the cavern, into a narrow passage. The air felt tight around them and their singing fell flat and empty against the close walls.

Blindly, they stumbled on. Johin still did not dare to open her eyes, and she gripped Manny's shoulder until her nails cut him deeply. He did not complain, but with one hand in front of his face to protect himself from unseen rocks, and the other hand holding the stump of the torch, they stumbled on into the dark, the ever-night where daylight had never been.

'What if we never see Nuffle again?'

'We will.'

'How do you *know?*'

'I know.'

'Why did he run off like that? Where is he?'

'He loves the River too; he can feel it calling him. He doesn't get distracted by thoughts like we do. He doesn't worry about *where* he is going, he just follows his heart. He didn't look at the crack in the rock and think, "It's dangerous down there", he just knew that was where he had to go. The River is calling him.'

'Is it calling you?'

'Yes.'

'Is it calling me?'

'Yes. Can't you feel it?'

'Yes.' Johin paused, then asked, 'Aren't you scared?'

'Terrified.'

'Why don't you show it?'

'Don't I? Perhaps you will see it later. If you do see me scared, will you promise me something . . .?'

'What?'

Manny hesitated. 'Will you keep singing for me . . .? And keep believing in the Light in the River, whatever happens?'

Johin did not like to think of Manny being scared, or needing her to sing for him. 'I promise,' she muttered.

Then there was silence and they slipped and crawled, walked and wriggled, through the narrow passage that led to the dripping trickling of the River and its source.

'How long have we been walking?'

'Hours.'

'Where are we?'

'Very deep.'

'It's silly to go into caves. We might never get out.'

'Yes, but this is different. This is the only time when it is right to go wriggling about in one.'

'I'm never going to do this again.'

'Good. Don't. Ever.'

Silence.

Suddenly Manny's hardened foot dislodged a stone. It fell. It bounced. It ricocheted down, and down, into the blind dark.

The final crack of the last landing of a new stone in a strange place, came a very long time later. Long, long seconds later. In the darkness, Johin collided with Manny's back again, and this time, it was the torch that fell, and fell.

They sat in silence as the pitch black night closed in around them. It was so velvety and soft, they began to be lulled into feeling that whatever they did, the gentle darkness would hold them, comfort them, and wrap them in deep black safety. It would carry them.

Manny jerked upright, 'No!' he shouted fiercely. 'No! We will not fall asleep! You will not kill me here!' and he started to scratch around furiously.

'What are you doing?' demanded Johin.

'Quick!' he demanded urgently. 'All the tiny pebbles you can find! . . . Now listen, listen deep inside yourself to the River. We have come the right way, yes?'

'Yes . . . I think so.'

'We'd know if we were wrong.'

'Are you sure?'

'Yes, it's *my* River. I'd know if I wasn't near it.'

'I wish you'd designed a better way in, then,' muttered Johin.

Manny laughed heartily. 'Yes, it could have been better!'

Johin poked him in his skinny ribs. A frightening thought had suddenly struck her. 'If this *is* your River, why don't you know the way? Why can't you find the way in? We're lost, aren't we?'

'Who said I can't find the way? It's just that thousands of years of water and earthquakes have turned it into an obstacle course . . . and I don't want to fall down *there!*' he said, dropping a pebble playfully down the gap.

She was silent for a little while. Then, 'I'm sorry about the torch,' she said morosely. 'Thank you for not shouting at me.'

'What good would that do? *I* was holding it. I was as much to blame for dropping it as you were. Anyway, we're almost there now.'

'How do you know?'

'Can't you *smell?*'

John sniffed. 'I can smell something rotten, nasty.'

'That's it.'

'The River?'

'No, the dump. I think we're almost below it. I told you the source is somewhere near the dump. We've just got to cross this hole. Now, be very quiet.'

In the stillness, Manny began tossing pebbles at different angles. Snap! snap! snap! they echoed into the depths, until at last one landed flat and dully, and skidded some way.

'That's it.'

'What is?'

'That's how far we've got to cross. Listen!'

The pebbles were landing on a firm surface not far away. 'The gap is about the length of a man,' said Manny cheerfully. 'Not far.'

'I can't jump that!' protested John. 'No way!'

'You may not have to. Stay absolutely still. Don't move a whisker. I'm going to try to find a way to climb round this hole.'

'Talking of whiskers, I wish I had Nuffle here,' said

Johin glumly.

Manny pushed one hand in front of the other, feeling along the rocky floor until his fingertips slid over the edge of nothingness. Carefully he groped first to the left and then the right. The crack opened out into a long slit that droped sheer between the walls of the tunnel. There were no footholds whatsoever. Manny flopped back next to Johin and sighed.

'Am I allowed to cry yet?' she asked, almost laughing, although she didn't know why.

Manny pushed his head back against the rock walls. 'No, not yet. Do you have the bottle of water from the Pool?' Johin shook it. Apart from Manny's voice, it was the only comforting sound in the whole place.

'Strange,' she said, 'it doesn't sound so full today.'

'Take a drink, and give the rest to me,' he said.

She did so, groping to find him in the dark. 'Got it?'

Manny drank. 'Yes, it is nearly empty. That means we are almost there. We'll have no more need of it once it's all over.'

'Will we get out of this alive?' she asked, suddenly really afraid.

Manny wiped a dry hand across his face. 'Yes, you will.'

'And you?'

'We'll see,' was all he would say. Then he was silent, as he busied himself with splashing and rattling water and stones.

'What are you doing?' she asked.

'I'm doing some Making.'

'Making?'

'That's what the water from the Pool is for, isn't it?'

'What do you mean?'

'I'm using water from the Pool to reshape the rock into a ledge for us to walk along. It won't be very big—there isn't much water, and I don't want to use all my strength. But it should be enough . . . Stay there, I'm going to try it out.'

She could hear him breathing heavily with effort as he heaved himself into the emptiness. Then there was the sound of a jump, silence and a firm landing. 'It's OK!' he called triumphantly.

Johin stood frozen to the spot. 'You really are, I mean, you always said . . . How can you make rocks change?'

'Johin, trust me. Hold firmly to the rocks on your right, there are some good handholds. Push your left foot out . . . can you feel a little ledge? Good. Push your foot a little further, now, transfer your weight onto it. Now, bring your right foot across. Good. Now do it again.'

'Manny, Manny, I can't stop shaking!'

Manny leaned out until he gripped her arm. 'Now move, quickly. I've got you.'

He pulled her firmly towards him, and before she had time to think about how frightened she was, she was standing next to him, shaking violently.

She glared accusingly, although he could not see her fury. 'If you really *can* make rocks change, why didn't you just close the gap, if you are . . . you know, who you say you are, you could have done it! Why did we have to go through all that danger? How could you! Couldn't you see I was terrified!'

Manny took her shoulders firmly. 'Calm down, Johin. It's all right, you're across. There's not far to go now. Yes, I could have done that, but the rocks here are very weak. There will be another earthquake soon, a bad one. I did not want to destabilize things any more. A pull here might open something worse further on. I want to get you out of here alive. We have to move gently. Sheer power is rarely the best answer.'

Johin's shaking subsided.

'If it's any comfort,' Manny said, 'I'm frightened too. Now, it's not much further, really.'

The stench was very bad. It was sweet, and musty. It smelled worse than the bogs at the edge of Greenhevel lake. The air was putrid and heavy with decay. Manny felt his way carefully along the right hand wall, edging forward with his bare toes, in case there were any more surprises.

Suddenly they turned a corner, and the place blazed with light.

22
The Words of Unmaking

At first they did not recognize the light for what it was; they had been so long in the total dark.

Manny pushed Johin back into the channel they had just left. Gratefully, she hid in the deep shadow.

Manny walked forward and stood at the edge of the chamber. From the curve of the walls, it was probably round, and very big, with a swirled twist gouged deeply into the rock. It had once been the heart of a great whirlpool, but now it was piled and stuffed with rubbish.

There were metal things of every description, bones, bottles, jars, machines, chemicals leaking from corroded drums, huge broken wheels and fearsome-looking contraptions of unknown origin. Stacked and thrown, piled and flung, the seemingly endless heap climbed out of sight, up into to the roof.

They were beneath the City dump. Centuries of rubbish crushed into the natural hollow above had caused the ground to collapse. Everything had fallen into the cave.

From underneath it all seeped a tiny trickle of water. It was the source of the River: it was also the end of the River.

In the middle of the cave sat Brilliance.

His menace was now complete. His eyes laughed pure evil. The brightness from his garments filled every part of the cavern, the glory of the spoil was woven into the fabric of his robes. There were no shadows.

'I tried to put you off coming here, boy!' he spat, darting terrible lightning from his eyes.

Manny looked small, earthy and very vulnerable.

'But you knew I would.'

'Idiot! This is *my* kingdom.'

'You've tried to make it yours.'

'It *is* mine. I have been worshipped here, at the very source of your precious River, since time began.'

'I see the votive offerings,' said Manny calmly.

'This is my gold and my kingdom ... I hold the whole Planet at ransom. They have chosen me as their lord. It is all mine now! Unless I say so, they all die. Those that bow to me, I will let live. Those that don't ...' he drew a slow finger across his neck.

Johin shivered.

Brilliance grinned. 'Tonight, the River Planet becomes *MINE!*' he roared. 'I am its life and its breath. No one will choose the River. What have you done for them? They've begged you to help over the years, but you've not moved a muscle to ease their pain and thirst! You don't care about them.'

Manny did not move or speak.

'Yes, what has he done?' Johin found herself thinking. 'It's taken him long enough to come and help us.' She could see that Brilliance had a point. She moved a little nearer to see more clearly.

Manny stood still and dark against the flash and sparkle of Brilliance. Johin closed her eyes. Into her head came the song Manny had sung. She saw the Sand people who had rescued her when she was alone in the desert. She watched them sharing their last food with her, an angry, bitter stranger ... then little Misha offering her rotten drought fruit when she was so near to starvation

174

herself. Then there was the terrible Wanderer King who had seemed so evil, but had saved Johin's life.

No, the River hadn't deserted them. It had given the gift of hands.

Hands, hands everywhere, offering help and healing, hands of different colours and sizes. One little tiny hand, a mouse's paw, pink with a delicate sheen of white fur. Nuffle had done his part too.

Suddenly she jumped. Nuffle! It really was Nuffle, he had found her, and had crawled into her hand. He sat warm and soft in her palm. She closed her hand around him and looked up at Manny and Brilliance.

Manny was undoing the stopper on the leather bottle. He poured water from the Pool of Making into his hand and flung it at the huge mountain of rubbish. Before Johin's eyes it began to melt.

The Unmaking was not hot and burning, as Johin expected, but very soothing and cool. Even the huge pieces of iron melted in coolness, and slid quietly into the ground, pouring and trickling away, as quietly as a child slipping off to sleep.

Brilliance laughed, but sounded strained in his throat. 'You haven't got enough there.'

'There is always enough!' said Manny solemnly.

Suddenly, he flung the entire bottle into the heart of the rubbish. With a deafening roar, the cavern shook and rose and crashed. For a few seconds it was rent open to the sky. Johin huddled in a crevasse, clutching Nuffle to her chest. As the ground convulsed she saw the stars, the sun and the moon all at once. It felt as if the Planet was splitting. 'This is it,' she thought. 'We were seconds too late.'

Manny stood tall and full of power, with his feet planted on the terrible, melting mountain of evil.

Johin could see he was in greater pain than ever, but he

threw back his head in a song of triumph.

'Be Unmade!' he commanded.

The Planet seemed to be sundering at its very roots. The rocks around them were tossing and clashing in full fury.

In the centre of it all, in what seemed like a still, silent, timeless bubble, were Brilliance, Manny and Johin.

As if oblivious to the terrible turmoil around, Brilliance stood unmoved, defiant and foul.

As the final earthquake reached its climax, Manny collapsed, screaming in pain. He fell to his knees, clutching at his sides. The Planet's suffering was his suffering. The River's death would be his own death. Johin understood it all at last.

Brilliance smiled with satisfaction. 'You were too late, it seems.'

'I was not . . . too late . . .' gasped Manny. 'The River is now free.' As he spoke, the tiny trickle of water that seeped through the rock-strewn cave suddenly swelled into a clear, bubbling spring. Manny seemed to straighten, as if the pain was lessening.

'We'll see,' sneered Brilliance.

The foul remains of rubbish were almost gone. The spring looked alive. Brilliance stretched out a long golden hand over the water, and the ground split wide open. Deep below was a pit surging with fresh clear water, leaping and tumbling, bursting up into the chamber.

Brilliance laughed. 'Watch,' he said, and with a flick of his finger the water boiled, steamed and evaporated even as it surged up.

'Not only has your precious Planet been damaged beyond your repair, but the River is gone as well. Wherever water breaks to the surface, it will become nothing. That is my magic of Destruction. It is far stronger than your Unmaking. By it I rule. Yet even now, I will be reasonable. Should you surrender your River Light to me, to my total control, I will let your puny people live. I will be their King . . . Speak, what is your choice?'

Manny shook his head painfully. 'No,' he groaned. 'It belongs to the Maker. It is not mine to give.'

Once again, Manny fell crumpled and dry at the feet of Brilliance. It hurt Johin to watch his face. He was mouthing something to her. He was too dry to speak.

Suddenly she caught a whisper: 'Sing.'

'What shall I sing?' she whispered back, but she knew at once it was a silly question. She thought of the River, and her dream-song about the Light in the River, and she made up words, husky, choking words, but words that would not give up.

For the first time, Brilliance noticed her. His eyes darkened. He lowered his gleaming eyebrows and beckoned her. She could not resist.

'Let me make my point,' he said. 'Not even your precious friends want you . . . do you, girl?'

Johin threw her head back and sang more loudly, and more defiantly.

'I know exactly what people want,' laughed Brilliance. 'Unlike your precious River, which couldn't care less about the drought.'

Brilliance glared straight into Johin's face and lifted her chin with one glistening finger. His dark oppression billowed out at her, and suddenly Brilliance's cloak became all she had ever wanted: the pretty purple and blue fluffy blanket, then a lovely silk dress she had seen a rich lady wear . . . In his hands he held huge bunches of fresh, fat, moist grapes and water melons. The yearning was too great. She wanted them more than anything . . . even more than the River in all its flood . . . she would die without that fruit. Surely the River would understand how weak and hungry she was ... It must understand why ... She stretched out her hands for them. She almost touched them.

She could feel Manny looking at her, but could not meet his gaze. 'I'm sorry, I must have them,' she said.

She put Nuffle in her pocket, and took some grapes. Scarcely had they touched her lips, and rotting sweetness slipped over her tongue, than the timeless stillness of the moment was smashed in a cacophany of clashing rocks. Johin was thrown flat on the heaving floor.

She closed her eyes and remembered the wonderful taste of the River water when they had swum so deeply. How could she ever have forgotten? She spat the taste of rotting grapes from her mouth.

Brilliance crowed in exultation. 'Mine! She's all mine! I have won the River Planet!'

Johin felt so ashamed she could not even cry.

She found herself tossed next to Manny. She buried her face. She could not look at him.

'Now I have her obeisance, I will destroy her. It is said in your tales, is it not, that whoever denies the River must die?'

'It is,' murmured Manny.

'If you really loved her, great River Light, if you really cared, she would have been safe. She would never have been put in a position where she *could* have betrayed you. Your weakness, boy, was in letting her think for herself. You should have kept her in a glass cage, safe from the cruel world. Now, she is mine, and I demand my right to Unmake her.' Brilliance held out his hand expectantly.

Manny, with tears streaming down his face, crawled to where he had thrown the bottle, and placed it into the gleaming, golden, clawing hand of Brilliance.

'No,' Manny said quietly. 'I do not deny your right.'

Johin tried to turn her head away from the burning breath of Brilliance. Panic-stricken, she called out to Manny. 'You can't, you can't let him Unmake me!... I'm sorry, Manny, I was so hungry and thirsty... please, Manny, *NO!*'

Brilliance gleefully lifted the leather bottle very slowly, raising it above Johin's head, and began to sing a thick, loathsome chant, with ripping, slicing words, full of hate and death.

'Be destroyed,' he intoned, deliberately and brutally.

Johin looked up and watched as the very last few drops of water from the Pool slipped down towards her face. It all seemed to happen so slowly.

Manny, brittle as dry parchment, looked at her, and met her terrified eyes with his own green-blue gaze of deepest water. 'Trust me, Johin.'

Johin screamed, 'Watch out!'

The water caught Manny on his outstretched hand, and in a terrible blast of burning air, Manny was Unmade.

23
Nuffle's Surprise

Johin lay face down on the hot rocks as the yellow sand blew freely away. The cavern had been cracked open to the sky in the earthquake, and she was lying on the empty floor. The dump was gone, and so was the source of the River. Everything was dry.

Manny was gone. He had been dried to nothing because *she* had been hungry. The last drop of water on the Planet was gone. It was all because of her. If she had held out ... if only she had kept on singing ... Now, the Planet would die, because of her stupidity.

The sun pounded down on her back and neck. Desolate, raging heat, calling her to despair.

The last of the stinking rot was coolly trickling away into every crevice in the rock. Everything had been reduced to its elements, copper, iron, carbon ... The magic in the Pool of Making had made everything return to what it really was. All the Planet's destructive poisonous ruin was Unmade.

But so was the water—so was Manny. There was no hope left. Nothing.

A hot wind blew into the empty cavern, and burning air filled her lungs. Everything was still. Everything was dry. She was alone.

Next to her, where Manny had been, two tear marks darkened the dust. Where Brilliance had stood was a small glistening knob of gold-coloured stone.

Shouts from above made her look up.

Collim and several of the Sand people from the dump were leaning over the lip of the newly-formed pit. They were holding something long and snaking. Looking up, she shielded her eyes aganst the relentless sun, and watched the dark silhouette lashing against the sky. Suddenly it dawned on her. It was a rope. She jumped and caught the end, made sure Nuffle was safe in her pocket, and tied the end tightly around her waist.

As an afterthought, she picked up the golden rock—it intrigued her. It was hot.

She glanced back into the cave. Strangely, the two dark stains on the dust had joined, and were now a dark smudge, the size of a thumbprint. It seemed odd, even important somehow, but she shook her head and called to be pulled up.

Collim and the Sand people pulled and sweated, and at last Johin was able to get a handhold on the rocks, and climb out.

She set Nuffle free and hugged Collim. 'It's good to see you ... well ...'

Collim laughed. 'Myself again? Yes, it's good to be back to normal. A donkey's life is not one I'd recommend. Where's Manny? Is he down there still?'

Johin shook her head. 'No. He's dead. And the source of the River is dry.' Johin looked at Collim and made herself say, 'It's all my fault. The Planet will be ruined. Everything is lost. Manny almost won, but I let him down. There's nothing left of anything, except what you see.'

Collim sat down heavily, and hugged his knees. Johin told him what had happened. They were both silent for a very long time. The Sand people sat softly talking at a little distance.

Johin nursed her cut and bleeding feet, and wished she

still had her sandals. She would go and get them later. Now, she had no heart to do anything.

Collim knew he would have done no better had he been there. All they could do was to hope that the end would come quickly.

Collim picked up the stone John had found. 'Where did you get this?'

'Down there,' she pointed below. 'What is it?'

'Iron pyrites. Fool's gold,' Collim shrugged. 'It's useless.'

John chucked it back into the enormous crater. As it thumped to the ground it cracked open, and shot black cinders into the air. 'That's all Brilliance ever was,' she said quietly.

Collim got to his feet. 'I think we'd better get clear of here. We've just had a terrible earthquake, worse than any I've ever known. I was surprised to find you alive down there.'

'If it hadn't been for Manny, I wouldn't have been.'

As she turned to go, she scooped up Nuffle and peered down once more. Far below, where the dark smudge had been, a tiny gleam caught her eye. John shrugged and, heavy with grief, walked away.

Desolately they climbed back over the saddle of the hill and stood on top of the slope that overlooked Genadatown and Heylebul Island. To their left, the huge blank wall of cream concrete that had been the High Dam was cracked. Half of it had tumbled and collapsed, filling the river bed below with huge broken pieces of cruel-looking slabs. Anyone caught below that stood no chance.

Collim snatched at John's arm. 'Look!' he said.

The Sand people saw it at the same time, and leaped, screaming and shouting with joy, down the hillside. The earthquake had split open the huge golden cone of

Heylebul Island grain store. Genadatown people were swarming like black ants to gather sacks heavier than they could carry.

Suddenly there were screams, as the Water Guards began to shoot the plunderers. Then, waving sticks and rocks, the Sand people turned and ran towards their oppressors. There was more shooting and shouting. Then everything went quiet. Dead Water Guards lay bleeding over the golden grain.

But the celebrations of finding food died in the still air of the approaching night. The people were too thirsty to eat. They could not swallow a single grain. For the first time in living memory, there was enough food for everyone on the Planet, but it was inedible.

Weeping and howling filled the still night air.

In miserable silence, Johin and Collim returned to the hut that had been theirs. It was not beyond repair, but there did not seem much point in doing anything. Death for everyone was just a matter of time.

All they could do was to lie still and wait. Johin heaved with grief and guilt. Everywhere there were still, grey, huddled shapes, waiting to die.

Eventually, Johin and Collim crawled out of their hovel and climbed out of the town to where the air was a little fresher. There they sat, and for the last time, Johin sang.

She was too thirsty to sing for long, but the thought of the death of the Lightwater agonized within her.

Hour after hot, still hour went by. Night faded into day.

Stillness.

Even the flies stopped buzzing. Unmoving bodies lay waiting. Johin wanted to sing, but fear and thirst stuck in her swollen throat. Collim waited silently by her side.

Darkness fell again.

In the middle of the night, a little rustle and a squeak in

the corner of the hut woke Johin from a feverish sleep. She sat up and stroked her beloved Nuffle as he lay next to her. He was twitching strangely. 'Never mind, it won't be long now. It'll be all over soon,' she said softly.

Nuffle twitched again, and again.

Johin felt she ought to kill him to put him out of his agony, but she couldn't bring herself to do it. 'Why are you the only one who is fat?' she asked him quietly. 'Do you have a secret supply of food and water?

Nuffle shook his little fat body and lay still.

'That's it,' thought Johin, 'he's dead too now.' She stroked his back.

He wasn't dead, and something lay glistening by his tail. There was another, and a third. Nuffle heaved and heaved until six tiny, pink babies lay scrambling blindly for their first drink of milk.

Nuffle was a *she*.

John leaped up like a mad thing, shouting through painfully cracked lips, 'Water! Water! I've got to have water, Nuffle's had babies!'

The desolate sleeping forms murmured and stirred, but no one woke except Collim. He sat up and looked at the little things. He touched one lightly with a finger.

'Poor little mites,' he said. 'It would be kinder to kill them quickly. If anyone has water to spare, it won't be given to mice. It will go to the human babies who are dying out there.'

John staggered to the opening of the hovel and peered into the dark, sulking night.

'Manny . . . was it all for nothing? Why did you have to go through so much, only to have everything ruined by me?' She turned and peered into the gloom at the dry shapes of dying people.

She leaned her head against the rough corrugated iron wall, slung at a drunken angle against the roof which had slipped to the ground.

Tap tap ... tap ... tap ... tap tap tap ... She turned her head and looked outside. 'What's that?'

Collim came and stood with her at the doorway. 'Tap, tap, tap tap tap...' it sounded like tiny pebbles thrown onto a roof. There were no children playing outside tonight. There was nothing. Could it be distant guns? The sound was very close, and small.

A strange, heady smell rose from the ground, and the noise became louder and louder until it became a deafening rattle.

Collim stretched his hand out into the night air. 'I've heard that sound once before, when I was very small ...' he said.

'What is it, Collim? I'm frightened.'

'It's rain, Johin ... rain.'

Shouting and clapping rose from every hut in Genadatown. Every pot, pan and vessel that could hold water was hurriedly put out to catch the precious drops. Jubilant bodies lay face up in the mud, open-mouthed to drink the rain as it fell.

Johin too, sat outside, loving the gentle drumming of the rain on her back. Nuffle feasted on a handful of grain from Heylebul and a saucer of water. Her babies seemed to uncurl and grow by the minute.

Tiny rivulets of water tickled down the back of Johin's neck. The cool squidgyness of mud lay between her fingers and toes. She thanked the Lightwater and was glad, but she wished Manny were there to see it, and to know it hadn't all been for nothing.

24
The Beginning

The morning was the first that Johin had ever known to be cold and wet. Through the empty doorway, she could see the dull, grey sky, heavy with thick rain-clouds. Their soft texture was cool and delightful. She had never seen a sky overcast with anything except high sandstorms and dust. The deep grey and blue patches where the clouds were thickest hung low over the mountains, swathing the slopes in life-giving moisture.

From where she lay, under the thin, tossing roof, Johin could marvel at the streaking gusts of wind and water sweeping down the valley, sloping in thick deft lines from sky to earth. She lay in her corner of the hut for a long time, watching and listening to the perpetual music on the tin walls. She was mesmerized by the grandeur and power of life which was being thrown so abundantly out of the sky.

Eventually, hunger drove her to climb down to the lower slopes of Genadatown, where huge piles of grain had been stacked. Blankets and sheets of metal had been thrown over the precious heaps to try to prevent them being washed away. Johin filled her satchel with a sticky mess of soggy grain, and climbed back up to the hut.

No one knew how to light a fire in the rain. In every hut, grain and water were being pounded into a soft, chewy mess. It tasted awful, but it was free, and there was as much as anyone could eat.

After breakfast, John carefully put Nuffle and her babies into a small box stuffed with rags, and squeezed it into the satchel. She wanted to have both hands free for the climb up the steep, slippery path to the saddle in the hills. She must get her sandals back—old and worn as they were, she needed them. Her feet were hurting. Collim went with her.

Collim and John stood on the top, in the wind and rain. All the Planet seemed to be in turmoil. Their wet hair lashed their faces, and they were cold. The whole hillside seemed to be moving under their feet as rain poured over the surface of the ground and sheeted down to hollows and miniature valleys. Rushing streams and swirling pools filled every dip in the ground.

They walked and slid down the slope to where the dump had been. The enormous gaping pit, opened and cleaned by Manny's magic, was now a wide, deep cauldron—a swirling yellow whirlpool. Skirting the boiling water, they climbed the next hill and looked down onto the plain which only two days ago had been empty and dry.

Now, the roaring of the River was deafening, as it fought to clear itself of the huge open cave mouth. Yet above it all was the tumultuous sound of laughter and singing.

The valley was running with Mud people, Sand people and Wanderers. Many of them were children, but even the older people were playing like six-year-olds. Some were water-tobogganing on their bottoms down the slopes into deep muddy puddles. Others were wallowing in mud, covering themselves so completely that they looked like fearsome monsters. Some were playing 'catch' and dunking their victims in yellow mud baths. Hoots of laughter, shouts and screams matched and rivalled the roar of the water.

The fast, swirling torrent of the River seemed familiar to Johin. She had seen it in the dream-song, the night Manny had sung part of the Song of the Lightwater.

Knee-deep in a muddy pool halfway down the slope on their left was a tall, thin figure with a mop of full brown curls. His head was thrown back, and he was laughing, with all the laughter of the world in his face.

Johin caught her breath. 'Manny? . . . How?' Part of her wanted to hide before he caught sight of her, but the other part of her wanted more than anything to run and hug him.

Manny turned and looked at her, and quietly held out his hands. He was no longer laughing, but he was still glad to see her. How could he *not* be angry when she had ruined everything?

Yet it wasn't ruined . . . it was raining, and there was Manny . . .

Johin wedged Nuffle's box against a sheltering rock, and with no thought for dignity she ran and ran, slipping, rolling and sliding on the mud chute until she lay at Manny's feet, smothered and filthy.

'Manny, I'm sorry, I'm so sorry!' she tried to say, but her mouth was full of mud.

Manny pulled her up and pushed her wet hair out of her eyes. He traced his Mark freshly on her head.

'I know,' he said. 'It's all over now.' His eyes looked so alive and glad, she felt glad too.

'How is it that you're . . . all right?' she asked hesitatingly.

Manny smiled. 'When I was Unmade, I became what we all are, sand—or mud—and water. But the Light's compassion for the River Planet and its people could not be Unmade. What you now see as "me" is the River Lightwater and sand—just as I always was.'

'You're real, then?'

'Yes.'

Johin surged with gladness. All she wanted was to laugh, and to jump up and down in the mud, and to roll down the hills with the children. Suddenly everything was alive and exciting and fresh and new.

Collim was trying hard to follow Johin down the slope, but could not abandon himself quite so totally. He stepped gingerly from stone to stone, until he stood carefully on a boulder at the edge of the impromptu quagmire. He was grinning—he desperately wanted to see Manny too. He wanted to say sorry for being such a donkey. He wanted to be glad, like Johin.

Manny looked at Collim and laughed again.

'Come on in, it's only mud!' he roared.

Collim looked down warily.

Manny stooped, and with one deft stroke bowled Collim over with a mud pie in the chest. Collim staggered, slipped, flapped his hands in the air like a wounded duck, and fell backwards with a luscious splat into the mud. He sat up, furious and dripping, looked down at himself, and felt the slow, cool oozing of mud seeping up his legs and inside his tunic. Then he threw back his head, and laughed. He raised one hand in defeat—but the other threw a mud ball that caught Manny fair and square on the back. Suddenly, it was a free-for-all. The most glorious mud fight of all time.

By mid-morning, the clouds had parted, and the sun came out. Not the raging, angry sun that Johin had known all her life, but a kinder, watered sun, one that gave life and warmth. Already grass was showing through the mud, and the steep valley sides had a thin film of shimmering green.

Exhausted, the muddy players lay back in the sun to rest. Some of the children started to twist their muddied hair into spikes, and let it harden in the sun. Johin twisted

Collim's hair into a huge spider shape.

When he felt the arrangement, Collim rubbed a thick handful of mud into Johin's face, and rolled her down the hillside into the pool, where she lay still and happy in a bath of untold squelching joy.

Collim shook his head until his long hair stuck out all over like a huge brush. 'I'll get you!' he warned with a grin.

Manny who had been silently watching, suddenly laughed aloud. 'You've given me an idea,' he said. 'The land has been bare and dry for so long, we need new animals and plants to help the Planet come to life again!' He pointed to the shallow pool that had been used for the mud fight. 'Make them in clay from here. Be wise makers as you were meant to be!'

Soon little forests of minature clay trees and animals were springing up around groups of chattering friends.

While the people were intent on their making, Manny called Johin and Collim, a few of the Sand people and a couple of Wanderers to walk with him. 'In the years to come, you must bring people here to see this place, and you must tell them the story of how the River died, and how it was remade. They must know of the magic of Unmaking, and Remaking. You must tell them, in case they forget and the Planet should die.

'When Brilliance Unmade me, he also started the ancient magic that will one day also Unmake him. In the real Light, you saw him for what he was, an imitation—fool's gold.

'His sway over the Planet's people is broken, but he is not dead. His going will need a slow, strong Unmaking that will take until the end of time to complete. The Maker's Light within the River is in your hands. You must be a part of Brilliance's Unmaking.

'It is a day by day "choosing and doing" sort of magic. Let the Lightwater flow, and it will work in you, if you use it well.'

Manny picked up a newly-made clay bowl, and filled it with water from the new Pool of Making. Walking slowly, he sprinkled the forest of silent clay trees, birds and animals.

Where the water splashed, the shapes shook and trembled, the clay cracked, and colours and textures of every kind spread and deepened across the living shapes.

Golden fur and purple feather, gleaming blue and green leaves, emerald scales and crimson hair glistened. Bright eyes winked and blinked. Heads shook the mud away, and long backs stretched. Mouths opened and yawned, and a delightful cacophany of squeaks and growls, grunts and twitterings sprang out of the silence.

Trees spread and opened like huge green and blue umbrellas above the people's heads, casting cool shadows on the young grass. And the air was filled with a soft scent of wet earth and new growth.

In the middle of it all, ran a little mouse with a long pink tail. A single drop of crystal water landed on the end of her shaking nose. It hung there for a second, glistening in the light. The little mouse wiped it off with a silky pink paw. Her ruby eyes twinkled as Johin ran to pick her up.

'Look, Collim,' she called, 'Nuffle's got silver whiskers. Manny always said she would!'

'Manny! Manny!' she called. 'Come and see this!'

But Manny was deep within the new forest with his bowl of water from the Pool. Pushing poor, patient Nuffle into her pocket once again, Johin ran after him.

Soon Manny and Johin had completely disappeared among the trees. In the cool greenness they sat down by a small stream. 'I want to go home,' Johin said quietly. 'Will you come? I miss my Mum and Dad. There's so much I want to tell them . . . but I don't want to leave you either.'

'I will always be around. Just listen.'

'But you're ... all right again. So why can't you come home with me?'

Manny leaned forwards and dabbled his hands in the water. 'I'll never be far away, unless you don't want me ...'

Johin winced at the memory of being alone in the desert.

Manny stood up and stepped into the stream, and turned to smile at her. 'Just listen, and watch; I'll be there. I'll miss you, so come and talk with me often—every day. But I won't ever be quite like this again.'

Taking his little clay bowl, he stooped down to the water, and filled it.

'Let's share good water together,' he smiled. 'Then the River will be in both of us.'

He drank and passed her the bowl.

Just as Johin drank, there was a tickle on her shoulder. Nuffle wanted her share. Johin placed the little mouse on the rim of the bowl, so she could drink.

When Johin looked up, Manny was gone. But the stream was singing gladly.